# ODIN

## The Diary of a CIA Assassin

by
Hank Anlaf and
Oscar Sannar

HATS
OFF™

Published in cooperation with
Rogue elephant Books

Published by Hats Off Books™
610 East Delano Street, Suite 104
Tucson, Arizona 85705

ISBN: 1-58736-270-8
LCCN: 2003097291

For questions about or comments on the contents of this book, or for permissions, please contact:
rogueelephantbooks@yahoo.com.

*For he is God's servant to do you good.*
*But if you do wrong, be afraid,*
*for he does not bear the sword for nothing.*
*He is God's servant, an agent of wrath*
*to bring punishment on the wrongdoer.*

*(Romans 13:4)*

# 1

## WARLORD

28 March 1995.

I looped the garrote over Kintu's head and hauled back. As the wire sliced into his neck, he let out a gurgle, so I crossed my hands, closing my weapon like scissors, and choked off his feeble protest.

A moment later the once-fearsome warlord went limp, dangling on my garrote like a clubbed marlin on a fishing line.

A scant year before, my target had been a Hutu commander, a beast in man's clothing who had blazed a crimson trail through Rwanda's Tutsi tribal lands. In his wake, Kintu had left a tangle of corpses—men, women, and children slain only for their rival bloodline.

And these victims died alone, without advocates, in the void that is Africa, until Odin, with my ears, heard the faint echoes of their screams.

Earlier on the evening of Kintu's death, and for the second time in as many weeks, I ushered across the warlord's threshold a quartet of prostitutes— young and rangy Abyssinians with skin like melted chocolate. Leering at the women, he grunted his approval.

"As always, dear sir," I said, "you have first pick."

Kintu strode over to the harlots, their willowy figures struck in come-hither poses, and said, "You spoil me, Reggie."

Two of these gazelles, I knew, would soon endure a night of abusive coupling with my newfound friend. From what I had observed at our first soirée, he'd likely developed his technique while razing Tutsi villages.

Behind the mask of Herr Johanns, bereft of fortune but still proud, I watched with apparent indifference as the Hutu commander hooked his arms around a pair of stunning lasses.

"Leave us," Kintu told his hovering bodyguards.

Assuming the role of host in another man's house, I began to ply the girls and the Hutu with heavy doses of liquor and Quaaludes from the commander's private stash. My aim was twofold: to anesthetize Kintu's chosen partners for what nastiness awaited them, and to render my target less of a threat to me.

In the small hours of the morning, after everyone else had indulged to excess and succumbed, I crept over to the commander, who lay sprawled on the thickly carpeted floor with his conquests. Shaking him awake, I noticed a round bloodstain on the rug next to one girl's nose.

What a pity.

Once Kintu's yawing and pitching eyes steadied on mine, I whispered, "Something very important. I must speak to you outside."

Five minutes later, standing on Kintu's expansive marble balcony, straddling his leaky carcass, I gazed awestruck at the moon's saffron swath across the sea. Then I dislodged my wire and, with a smear of blood, pasted a calling card on the butcher's shiny head.

\*    \*    \*

Two months earlier, as part of a sanctioned CIA operation in Rome, I created the persona of financially desperate Austrian nobleman Reginald Johanns. After receiving my alias documents from Agency Headquarters, I attempted to cozy up to the authorized target—a Montenegrin aristocrat involved in the illicit arms market—but realized no success of note. I must admit that I was never committed to the operation.

So instead, yielding to my private motives, I took a holiday to East Africa. And in my designer luggage I secreted Reginald's documents and my disassembled garrote.

Five hours after my arrival in Ethiopia, I locked my true-name passport in a hotel safe deposit box, transformed into Reginald, and crossed the border overland into Kenya as a member of a photo-safari. I later separated from the tour group and whiled away the remainder of my vacation on the country's beautiful coast.

According to CIA reports I'd read in Rome, the Hutu commander, fearing reprisal from a Tutsi army mustering in Uganda, had recently cashed in his plunder and bought a handsome exile in Mombasa, a Kenyan resort city. Using a local real estate agent, I tracked down Kintu's ocean-view condominium and signed a one-month sublease for a suite of rooms.

For the next two afternoons I paraded a pair of East African beauties—courtesy of Mombasa's best escort service—around the complex's swimming pool, right under the twitching noses of Kintu and his bodyguards.

On the third day, unable to contain himself any longer, the retired Hutu commander ambled over to my chaise lounge and said, "Can a man with such splendid diversions ever find time for a full-course meal?"

"With constant demands like these," I answered, stroking the slender thigh of the girl to my right, "one must take sustenance regularly, to keep up one's strength."

"May I suggest dinner tonight then?" He drank in the women with his eyes. "For all three of you, I hope."

"A most generous invitation, sir, but I'm afraid we must decline."

Kintu's face fell and then twisted into a comical pout.

"I cannot in good conscience leave my other companions to fend for themselves," I explained. "Exquisite ladies, local models—mostly lingerie, some swimsuits. Out shopping now, both of them, no doubt working up their appetites."

"The more the merrier," Kintu said, his voice little more than a growl. "Table for six, eight o'clock. I'm in the penthouse."

"Please excuse my bad manners." I pulled myself from the chaise and bowed my head in what I hoped passed for blueblood etiquette. "The name is Reginald Johanns, late of Austria, now of wherever the wind blows me. But you can call me Reggie."

Holding out his hand to me, but looking mainly at the girls, Kintu offered his expatriate alias: "Monsieur Dubois. Very pleased to make your acquaintance, Reggie."

I felt only revulsion as I grasped what had been the instrument of so much depravity and suffering.

But then I found great solace in the thought that Kintu—the mass-murderer, the rapist, the torturer—would soon become the eighth casualty of my one-man crusade.

★   ★   ★

An icy wave of foreboding washed over me, and I woke with a start, feeling anxious, addled. At thirty-seven thousand feet, I remembered, on an airliner, bound to Italy from Ethiopia. Now I had a fix on my position: Yesterday, far behind me in Kenya, I'd left a dead Hutu warlord.

"Can I get you anything, Mr. Anlaf?" a passing flight attendant asked.

"Vodka, please, neat."

I threw back the drink and it soothed me, but still I sensed a coming tragedy, a violent end to my run of good luck. Who knows, I asked myself, what might be waiting for me back in Rome? I could be dead in a few weeks, a few days, a few short hours.

Roused by this gathering storm, I reached for my fountain pen and notebook. Then and there I resolved to set down a chronicle of my exploits, a literary scream into the dulled ears of my masters—that evil bends *only* to virtuous wrath.

# 2

# SPARROW

30 August 1992—the beginning.

I landed in Manila on my third field assignment with the CIA. I'd just wrapped up four challenging years in the Near East—two in Islamabad, Pakistan, and another two in Damascus, Syria—and was eager to indulge in Manila Station's slower operational tempo, not to mention the country's comely women.

I'd also recently come to the distasteful conclusion that my organization's leaders were hopelessly petty and selfish, looking out only for themselves, their careers, and their fiefdoms. These men and women, I had observed, had reached their lofty posts through the frequent practice of sycophancy, calumny, and self-promotion—not by proving their professional competence.

My best friend, Stan Bauer, agreed with my assessment, but encouraged me to give the Agency one last try. Stan, who'd been in Manila for a year and was scheduled to stay for two more, begged me to request transfer to the Philippines until at last I gave in. I could never say no to Stan.

Stan and I had met in 1987 at XXXX XXXXX,* the CIA's training camp in southern Virginia. There, between the paramilitary training and tradecraft exercises, we had formed a fast friendship based on our similar yearnings to explore the dark and sultry parts of the world, our mutual interest in history and politics, and our insatiable appetites for sharing the company of exotic women.

★    ★    ★

14 October 1992.

I walked into the office I shared with Stan, sat down at my desk, and switched on my clunky Wang workstation. Stan, his face buried in a local newspaper, bid me good morning, and let out an admirable string of profanity.

"They're cutting the bastards loose," he said, finally able to form a full and coherent sentence. He threw the Filipino tabloid across the room, its pages fluttering like the wings of an injured bird.

I leaned back in my chair and gazed over at my friend, soliciting elaboration with raised eyebrows.

"Those murderers," he said, "the ones who killed the three sailors outside Subic Naval Base."

I shrugged.

"Jesus, Hank, didn't you read the backgrounder at Headquarters? The hit went down back in Eighty-eight. The marks were two active duty boys and one retired chief petty officer, all sitting in a burger joint near the main gate. A communist Sparrow squad does a drive-by and hoses down the three sailors—plus a few innocent bystanders. Any of this ring a bell?"

---

* Deleted at the request of the U.S. Government.

"You might've set off my tinnitus."

Frustrated, Stan let out a heavy sigh, then soldiered on: "A couple years ago, two of the shooters got collared and thrown in the pokey for life. Bravo, bravo. But now the papers are saying both sentences will be commuted, and that Fenil Manag is going to get amnesty *in absentia*."

"Manag? Never heard of him."

"The Sparrows' top scumbag, plans all their hits. Probably drowns kittens in his spare time. Meet up with him in a dark alley, you can kiss your ass goodbye."

Unaware he'd just divined my future, Stan shot me a look of mock reproof. Then he threw up his lanky arms, surrendering to my ignorance, swiveled around to his keyboard, and began pecking out a cable message on his Wang.

★   ★   ★

11 November 1992.

Not knowing me intimately, you might jump to the conclusion that Stan's simple rendition of this injustice was all that it took for me to assume the life of a covert mercenary. But you must understand that I was not then the man I am now; I have transformed over the years into that unrepentant hangman who later dispatched the Hutu warlord on a one-way trip to Hell. Back when I began my tour in Manila, I was relatively unsullied and still needed to feel the cold sharp steel of evil before I committed to my coarse endeavor, which I now recognize as my unavoidable destiny.

I experienced my inaugural violence secondhand, though the resulting loss was highly personal and ignited within me a fury as if I myself had borne the physical brunt of the attack. It was my dear friend Stan whose blood was spilled, whose body was mangled, whose altered life spawned vengeance in my heart.

Stan's life was forever changed as he walked from the Embassy's Chancery to his car, which was parked in the lot adjacent to Manila's busy Roxas Boulevard. By my reckoning, a week more or less had passed since our talk about the Sparrows' being granted amnesty.

Later, the Embassy's local-hire guards and Filipino investigators were able to reconstruct the attack. A commandeered jeepney, one of the country's gaudy, ubiquitous mini-buses, screamed down the sidewalk in front of the embassy, trailing a cyclone of propaganda leaflets, forcing pedestrians to leap to safety. The jeepney's driver, later identified as a known Sparrow operative, slammed on the brakes, bringing the vehicle to a screeching halt at the concrete base of the embassy's black iron perimeter fence.

The jeepney's passengers, shouting slogans about renewing the NPA's★ fight against American imperialism, leaned out and tossed five hand grenades over the fence. One detonated immediately, tossing the men back into the jeepney, three of the devices failed to blow, and the fifth skipped across the asphalt parking lot toward Stan, who was crouching, caught out in the open.

Turning away, Stan wrapped his arms over his head a split second before the grenade exploded approximately five feet away from him. The blast caught my friend full in the back and launched him across the lot into the embassy's neatly trimmed grass.

---

★ New People's Army, a communist group waging an insurgency against the Philippine Government.

Two brave U.S. Marine Security Guards emerged from the bulletproof safety of the Chancery and retrieved Stan's twisted rag-doll body.

Meanwhile, the jeepney driver had regained his senses, executed a U-turn, and sped away down Roxas, southbound. According to several witnesses, the local-hire guards, armed with shotguns and revolvers, watched the whole incident with mouths agape and failed to fire a single shot.

Who could blame them? It must've been quite a show.

★   ★   ★

23 November 1992.

My direct supervisor, a branch chief named Margaret, waddled into my office, and in an apathetic monotone rattled off an update: "Stan's American physicians agree with the prognosis of their Filipino colleagues. He's permanently paralyzed from the waist down."

A shard of shrapnel, a quarter-sized section of the grenade's steel casing, had plunged into Stan's lower back, carving away a chunk of his spinal cord. He was evacuated to the States a week after the capable doctors at Makati Medical Center had stabilized him.

Though her expression was sullen, Margaret's eyes blazed with excitement, betraying her true feelings—she enjoyed being the harbinger of bad news.

"So what's our response?" I asked.

"I'm not following you."

"What's CIA going to do—bring in a Special Activities team, request help from Delta Force?"

Margaret held up her hands, palms toward me, and shook her head. "Slow down, Hank. We're talking about a sovereign nation here. No way we're going to send a unilateral unit in to hunt these guys down. And I doubt the Filipinos will invite our assistance, or even lift a finger on their own. The GOP* won't do anything now for fear of derailing the armistice talks with the Party. This is a very delicate time for them on the domestic front."

Margaret pursed her thin lips, shrugged and glanced heavenward with great drama, then lumbered away.

Furious, and a little nauseated, I desperately needed to focus on something other than poor Stan's plight, but on my desk was an evidence bag, recently delivered from the Philippine National Police. I opened the thick plastic pouch and reviewed its contents—a bundle of the terrorists' fliers, scattered along the sidewalk before the attack. The leaflets thanked the Philippine government for Sparrow leader Fenil Manag's pardon and implored the downcast Filipino masses to rise up and drive the American imperialists from the workers' homeland. The concluding sentence promised a new wave of violence against U.S. interests in the Philippines, a never-ending string of assaults more vicious and far-reaching than ever before experienced.

My heart raced and my skin grew hot and sweaty as my rage neared critical mass. Swirling about in my head was a maelstrom of thoughts about the unconscionable pardons, about my own government's frailty and unwillingness to force the Philippines back onto a righteous course, about the end-game of these feeble moves: the barbaric, unanswered vivisection of Stan's hopes and dreams.

---

* Government of the Philippines.

And I snapped. In my skin, looking out through my eyes, the snap was audible.

Until that very moment I didn't know how close I'd been to my breaking point, how deeply the near-fatal attack on Stan had stung me, how frustrated I'd grown with the CIA's neglect of its basic mission—to protect, from the frontline trenches of espionage, our proud and prosperous nation.

Then, suddenly illuminated before me in a shower of blinding silver-white light was my true path, from which only timidity or cowardice could divert me. The revelation was divine, the most sacred moment of my life.

The good people of the world, being wronged every second of every day, would now be avenged. And I would embark on my consecrated mission by excising that black tumor known as Fenil Manag.

★   ★   ★

Passion sometimes bleeds into rage, which dances around the margins of madness.

Had my fervor crossed the line into delirium? Or did I remain lucid, still capable of reason and sound judgment? At that moment, sitting in my office, evidence bag in hand, God speaking in my ear (which alone can rupture a flawed soul), I was no longer sure about my sanity—or about anything else.

For years I'd stifled my fiery criticisms of the CIA. I'd seen too many bootlickers rewarded, too many righteous missions abandoned, too many essential duties neglected. Now my best friend was a victim of this ineptitude, this corruption, this apathy.

Intolerable.

Inexcusable.

Reproachable.

Consequences be damned: It was time for me to take matters into my own hands.

# 3

# BELLWETHER

14 December 1992.

I began my mission—which, though personal, was for the good of all humankind—by reviewing the Station's reporting on the New People's Army. We had several penetrations of the NPA and its political counterpart, the Communist Party of the Philippines, but only one of our agents had direct and complete access to Fenil Manag—his personality, his relationships, his movements.

This agent's code name, stripped of its country-specific prefix digraph and suffix series number, was Bellwether. Much to my chagrin, Bellwether's finest contributions, including key details on Comrade Manag, were hidden in a compartmentalized computer database, to which only the Chief of Station, his deputy, and Bellwether's handler, a young first-tour officer named Debby Winfield, had right of entry.

Removing the Deputy Chief of Station, I realized, would get me nowhere; I was too junior to succeed him. I was left with only one viable option: I had to take Debby out of the starting lineup. The question was, *how*?

The answer was in tealeaves. Debby, I discovered, drank a quart of premium black pekoe every day, both in sickness and in health. In sickness, I thought; well, glory be.

At first I worried that Debby might taste the strong purgative* I'd mixed into her precious leaves, but I needn't have fretted, for Debby's palate proved to be as dull as her humor. Three hours after slurping down a tainted cup, she succumbed to a mysterious intestinal malady, and for an entire month, until her tea tin was bare, Debby never once strayed more than a few feet from a serviceable commode.

Of course I was quick to lend a hand, offering to pick up my poor colleague's caseload until she finally recovered from her odiferous ailment. My ostensible charity brought me full access to the wonderful Bellwether database, in which I found the portent of a most needful death.

★　　★　　★

18 December 1992.

Fenil Manag was obsessed with gambling, and in the great game of espionage, obsession equals weakness, for it overcomes a person and deprives him of rational thought. Bellwether, who grasped the significance of this frailty, had offered a full report on Manag to Yankee Doodle Debby.

Though she lacked an appreciation for venality, my dutiful coworker recorded all of Bellwether's insights, most likely while holding her nose. But Debby delved no deeper, asked no follow-up questions, and thus failed to collect any actionable intelli-

---

*According to Mr. Anlaf, in the early 1990s many controlled pharmaceuticals could be purchased in the Philippines without a prescription.

gence on Manag's character—the finer points of his passions, his impulses, his addictions.

That all changed when I grabbed the reins. I wasted no time devouring the case file, carefully sorting out the few useful grains from Debby's bushels of chaff. Only a productive face-to-face meeting with Bellwether, I concluded, would provide the missing tactical tidbits required for my plan.

$$\star \quad \star \quad \star$$

21 December 1992.

On the very day that I was handed the Bellwether case, I walked out and made a simple chalk mark on the appointed concrete pillar in an underground parking garage, signaling for a rendezvous with our premier agent. In keeping with an established protocol, two days later, at nine in the evening, I picked up Bellwether in my car and debriefed him on the roll, using a long list of collection requirements from Headquarters.

(My brisk, decisive approach stood in stark contrast to the CIA's standard operating procedure, which called for a bevy of officers to dissect any proposed action until it was rendered impotent or, through interminable delays, obsolete. Nothing baffled me more than the fact that risk, a natural byproduct of operations, was anathema to CIA.)

Bellwether was shy but amiable. According to his file, he was also a courageous soldier. As a young field lieutenant a decade before, he'd led his men on hundreds of wildly successful ambushes against the Philippine Army in the jungle-clad hills of Samar Island. Several promotions followed. Then Bellwether was asked to join the NPA's senior leadership, where he served with distinction as a military strategist and Party theorist.

But in his private life the warrior was an incurable Milquetoast. His domineering wife—by his own admission a clone of his mother—had henpecked him into submission, relentlessly dousing him with her vitriol, recounting how his "ideals" had impoverished the family.

Nearing the end of his rope, with nowhere to turn for help, Bellwether had forsaken everything in which he had ever believed and scampered over to the enemy camp. Once he'd proven himself reliable, the CIA money had flowed deep and wide, allowing him to finance his son's education at Cal Poly and, as a marvelous bonus, to stave off the incessant carping of his spouse.

But by the time this reprieve came, the damage was already done: Bellwether's fascist wife had worn him down, broken his spirit. Throughout the case file, Agency handlers described him as "resigned and compliant."

I too found Bellwether passive. He regarded me with weary disinterest when I swerved away from the list of prepared questions and for the next half hour probed into Manag's habits and activities, day by day, hour by hour.

"For the past three months," Bellwether said in his unnerving deadpan timbre, "on Thursday nights at ten o'clock, Manag slinks away from whichever NPA safehouse he happens to be staying in. He leaves behind his bodyguards, goes to Chinatown, and stays for two hours, sometimes a little longer."

"A craving for kung-pao chicken?" I asked.

"A craving, yes, but not for food. He sits in on the city's best high-stakes blackjack game, which for years has been held in a tenement at the corner of Claro Recto and Juan Luna. If he wins, he celebrates by renting time with the house's newest and youngest male prostitute, taking the unlucky boy for a couple rough-and-tumble victory laps. If not, he goes straight home to his wife. Emphasis on 'straight.'"

"I thought the Party prohibited its members from taking part in homosexual practices."

Bellwether chuckled, which was, for me, a welcome change from his usual wooden demeanor. "The Party forbids corruption too," Bellwether said, "but the Chairman has been skimming for years. Everyone knows that. Manag is a hero. The Party has a blind eye for every occasion."

★   ★   ★

7/14 January 1993.

As always, Bellwether's reporting was spot on. For two consecutive Thursdays, I sat down the street from the dilapidated apartment building in one of the Station's ops cars, fabricated "Awaiting Registration" plates on its bumpers, wearing a suffocating mask that made me look like a Filipino. I smelled like rum, had empty bottles on the floorboard, and appeared to be passed out behind the wheel. My alias driver's license and pocket litter identified me as Teofisto Nuñez, the owner of a print shop that just happened to be a vacant lot in a very bad part of Manila.

Through hooded eyes I watched Fenil Manag slither into the darkened tenement at ten-twenty both nights, out the first evening at half past midnight, and out again the second at two o'clock, after apparently having celebrated his good luck at the table. I recognized the homicidal mastermind from his mug shot on an old Philippine National Police "wanted" poster.

The streets were empty for both of his departures. The neighborhood's Chinese merchants always closed and shuttered their shops before sunset, acquiescing until dawn to the influx of sedition and crime.

I welcomed this nocturnal hand-over: What was bad for the conduct of commerce would be good for a bloody act of retribution.

★   ★   ★

21 January 1993.

I brought my CIA-issued Browning Hi-Power pistol to the very next Thursday stakeout. My weapon was loaded with hollow-points, which I'd asked my father to purchase in the U.S., conceal in the base of a brand-new metal reading lamp, and ship to me through the embassy's mail system.

"Full metal jackets aren't worth a crap," I'd told him during an international telephone call. "It takes a whole magazine just to piss off a bad guy. I need something that slips in, plays a fierce round of pinball, and leaves behind a fist-size souvenir."

This was a ruse, of course, for the sake of parental peace of mind—to reassure my father that I was looking out for my personal safety. My actual concern was that Agency-issue rounds might be traced back to the U.S. Government, and such an outcome would surely precipitate a serious diplomatic scandal. The last thing I wanted to do was drag my dear old Uncle Sam into any of my private skullduggery.

But I needn't have worried: My father did right by me, sent enough of America's finest cop-killers to fill a spare magazine. He knew that any point worth making was a point worth repeating.

Manag departed the apartment building a quarter after twelve, apparently having no excuse to indulge in any man-boy love, and walked down the street toward a parked car. According to Bellwether, one of Manag's sympathetic NPA buddies lent him a vehicle every week, always perversely eager to help feed a comrade's addictions.

My plan was simple: The fewer moving parts, the less chance of breakdown. Or so I thought. I climbed out of my car, my arm tucked under my stained and baggy shirt, my hand gripping the cocked-and-locked Browning, and strode double-time after Manag.

The first thing I noticed was Manag's size: He was big—a detail I'd missed from my observation post at the far end of the street. Drawing within a hundred feet of my target, I could see beneath his tight T-shirt a set of broad shoulders brocaded with muscle and sinew. By the time I'd halved that distance, his frame was looming over me like a windjammer's mainmast and yardarms. I began to feel a gnawing sensation in my gut.

Surprise—that was what I needed. I kept telling myself that I *had* to take my target by surprise. His bulk and strength wouldn't matter if I caught him unawares. Just walk up and cap him, right in the back of his big Filipino melon.

Manag's head ticked to the side, suggesting to me that he'd heard my footfalls. But he didn't turn around. I instantly altered my plan: Instead of gunning him down point-blank, I'd empty my weapon into him from, say, two yards back. I noticed that I was already more or less within that range, so I extracted my pistol and swung it to the ready.

In a flash, Manag pirouetted, lunged, and smashed my arm, sending me stumbling across the filthy sidewalk. I bounced off a storefront and watched a cascade of blinking lights stream past my eyes.

Manag came at me again, hurling a vicious right cross, an arcing smudge of speed, my face centered in its trajectory. I parried, but the blow grazed my crown, rousing on my tongue a taste of metal, and in my mind an image of splintered thermometer glass, pooled mercury.

Still on my feet but barely, I obliged my lack of balance and let it spin me around until I found myself off Manag's port gunwale. That was when I noticed I was still holding my pistol, tucked in close to my hip. I squeezed off two rounds, didn't bother to move the gun, didn't aim at all.

I'm unsure if I hit Manag—I doubt that I did—but he jumped back just the same, probably startled by the sharp blasts that echoed through the neighborhood. But his surprise faded quickly, and he charged me, jabbing with his left, a steam hammer coming out of the dark. His fist breezed by my chin and landed squarely on the crook of my left arm, spinning me around and lifting me up onto the balls of my feet.

In a bolt of belated comprehension, as I floated back down to Earth, I realized that I was about to get the holy shit beaten out of me. Worse yet, this baboon would probably finish me off with my own gun, and my riddled body would be found the next morning wearing that goofy CIA mask. No way was I going to let that happen. So as fast as I could squeeze the trigger, I began spraying hot lead in the general direction of my opponent, hoping that at least one round would connect.

At least one did, and Manag went down hard as if I'd swiped him with a chainsaw at the knees. But he was still alive—groaning, muttering, writhing, and holding his oozing gut. I took a step toward him and waited for his eyes to focus on me. When our gazes locked, he raised his eyebrows and snickered, probably at my ridiculous mask, which was now slightly askew, thanks to his pummeling. (I seem to recall that my left eye was peering out through one of the nostril holes.) I couldn't let such slapstick be this killer's last view of the world, so I ripped off the disguise, revealing my lily-white visage. That shut him up *tout de suite*, and his glittering little eyes grew big as saucers.

I said, "Payback for Stan Bauer, Comrade," and I fired my pistol until its slide locked back—four rounds, I think. I loaded my spare magazine and emptied it into the dead man's chest (pirate pun intended), sending a clear message that scum like Manag had better crawl back under their rocks or risk meeting a similarly messy demise.

Just in case you're wondering, the answer is no— I felt no contrition for snuffing out this vermin's lousy spark of life. I felt only rapture from having authored an exquisite revenge.

\*    \*    \*

29 January 1993.

All artists sign their creations. I knew that, and I kicked myself for not claiming my handiwork. It was my first kill, after all, my initiation into the priesthood of assassination. The event was an important milestone. I would be better prepared next time, I promised myself that.

From a storage trunk in my apartment, I liberated the results of research I'd done years before. At the time, I'd been looking for a stylish design that I could have pricked into my skin. I was briefly beguiled, I must confess, by the art of tattoo but snapped to my senses just short of the needle.

Leafing through my sketches, I came across a stylized raven, a symbol of the Viking god Odin, traced from a museum photograph of a thousand-year-old Norse coin. The emblem seemed appropriate on two counts: Odin was known as the "Lord of the Slain," and the blood of Scandinavian immigrants coursed through my veins.

Yes, I decided, this would be the ensign of my cause; with this symbol I would mark my kills.

I then typed up an explanation of the symbol and a claim for the Manag hit, complete with details that only the killer would know. Late one night at the Embassy, I made six photocopies of my drawing and narrative, and addressed three sets to large Philippine newspapers and the other three to U.S. news-media outlets. On my drive home, I dropped each package into a different sidewalk mailbox.

This corrective measure left me with only one major exigency: I had no formal training in hand-to-hand combat. I would need to remedy this sad truth to prevent any repeat performances of my embarrassing skirmish with the brawny Mr. Manag.

I delved into exhaustive research on the topic, studying the efficacy of Japanese aikido, jujitsu, and karate, of Korean hapkido, tae kwon do, and taekkyon, of Chinese wing chun, chin na, and choy li fut. I even checked into more modern fighting systems, most of which were derivative of the Asian arts, such as the

U.S. Navy SEALs' SCARS method and Israeli Krav Maga.

Each of these disciplines had its strong points. Each was brutally effective in its own way. But the deciding factor for me was one of availability. You must remember that I still had two more years to serve in the Philippines.

Following a winding word-of-mouth trail, I stumbled upon a dojo in Manila that taught the ancient Japanese samurai art of Daito Ryu Jujitsu: no-nonsense joint locks, throws, and bone-breaking techniques blended with meditative exercises. According to Japanese martial dogma, this style's spiritual component was intended to calm the heart and mind, allowing highly trained adherents to enter unavoidable conflicts with serenity and calm, to make clear-headed decisions, and to apply their menacing skills with enlightened selectivity and justice.

Much to the detriment of my day job with the CIA, I threw myself into the study of Daito Ryu and, within a year, was awarded a first-degree black belt. My Sensei pronounced me a model student, well on my way to even more advanced study, already a master of the art's most abstruse techniques and concepts.

And I pronounced myself ready for my next secret assignment, which I would undertake after some prurient indulgence.

# 4

# DUTCH

16 February 1993.

I rang Stan at his parents' house in Sacramento, California, two days after his scheduled discharge from the hospital.

"Bauer here," he said after his mother handed him the telephone. His voice sounded strong, and my mood brightened.

"Stan the Man. Time to fulfill your wildest fantasies, my friend."

"If this is Hank, and if he's talking about the island, then he's out of his fucking mind. I can't even make my big toe twitch, good buddy, let alone my bigger toe. Deader than a doornail from the waist down."

This was bad news I'd already heard, though still no easier to take the second time around. But I would not be deterred. I fortified myself with a deep breath and continued: "Been talking to your doctor and he says your pecker still has some sensation, may very well stand up and salute one day, given regular exposure to fresh air and exercise."

"You talk awfully freely about my pecker, you pecker. Exactly what did you have in mind?"

"The island of Sparta, my friend, just as we planned. I hear tell you got your full pension, topped

off with a nice chunk of restitution for pain and suffering. I advise you to invest your newfound wealth
wisely. I have five young things already in the winner's
circle and another five nearing the finish line, all begging to take your dog for a walk each and every day."

Stan was guffawing now, and I heard his mother's
concerned voice in the background. "I'm fine, Mom,
really," he said, his voice directed away from the
mouthpiece. And then to me: "Good buddy, this rack-
et of yours has three important requirements: location, location, and location."

"Done, done, and more than done. Now roll your
crippled ass onto the next plane and let Hank take care
of the rest."

"Two more weeks of convalescence and medical
appointments, then I'm all yours. Of course, my folks
will blow a gasket when they hear I'm going back to
the scene of the crime."

"You tell them that Brother Anlaf will look after
you, along with my bevy of adept and nubile prose-
lytes, emphasis on nubile. Actually, equal emphasis on
adept. Nothing left to worry about here. Your partic-
ular nemesis is now taking the long dirt nap."

"So I heard, good buddy, so I heard."

\*    \*    \*

An excerpt from an old diary:
30 April 1987, graduation day.

The island, as a dream and as a goal, first surfaced
during our paramilitary familiarization course down
at the CIA's XXXX XXXXX,\* known to the blessed
few as The Farm. Stan and I, both adventurous and
unattached, stayed at The Farm every weekend in

---

\* Deleted at the request of the U.S. Government.

Quonset huts—alternately freezing and stifling—cloistered in the southern Virginia woods, while our classmates tripped over one another to get back to family and friends in the Washington DC area.

The coxswain for our chimerical voyage to the island was retired Master Sergeant Lester Ingram, U.S. Army Special Forces, whose exploits in Vietnam filled a worn and dog-eared chapter of CIA lore. The Master Sergeant, as the legend went, had a remarkable gift for tracking down and killing Victor Charlie. This talent for butchery, however, paled in comparison to his genius for sniffing out and seducing the prettiest lasses the Third World had to offer. (Of this latter claim Stan and I were soon to learn much more.)

At the end of the CIA's eight-week paramilitary course, we finally learned the Master Sergeant's given name. The revelation was his farewell present to us, his devoted disciples. Until then—and even afterward—we called him what everyone else did: Dutch.

From our first weekend at The Farm, leathery old Dutch took a real liking to Stan and me. The "stay-behinds," he called us, an obscure reference to agents and saboteurs left to operate alone in hostile territory during the advance of an enemy force.

Dutch routinely convened our triumvirate in a big hangar at The Farm's airfield, the locus of our course's Air Ops, where we packed bundles of supplies to be kicked out of low-flying airplanes to the "partisans," bands of our fellow classmates, on the ground below. In the shade of the hangar, primed with watery beer and pork rinds, Dutch regaled us with his full repertoire of stories—many too classified, or too libertine, to repeat.

Of all Dutch's chronicles, his description of the island was, to us, the most memorable. It left an indelible, haunting mark on the young minds of Stan Bauer and Hank Anlaf. Dutch's island redrew the boundaries of our reality, redefined our expectations, and implanted within us a new and most ferine purpose.

"Go out now and make your own island," Dutch whispered to us at graduation, a sheen of tears forming on his normally dry and scornful eyes.

★ ★ ★

Back in 1970, after pulling two voluntary tours of duty as a Special Forces buck sergeant in Vietnam, Dutch Ingram was detailed to the CIA, where he ran a section of the Agency's provincial tripwire intelligence network. After a couple of years of hamlet defense and search-and-destroy missions, Dutch found that working for the CIA was like going on an extended vacation. Even the schedule was sweet: two weeks on, two off.

One night over beers in a Saigon bar, Dutch and three other Special Forces buddies, all winners of the CIA Sweepstakes, hatched a scheme to occupy their newfound leisure time and to burn through their freshly fattened paychecks.

"I'll call my friends Curly, Moe, and Larry," Dutch said to Stan and me. "Those of them who're still alive have families, and those who're dead still have honor." Dutch hesitated, and he narrowed one eye, scrutinizing us.

"Come on, Dutch," Stan said. "You can trust us. We might plagiarize, but we won't tell a soul."

Dutch's face instantly softened, and he grinned and nodded. "A year before I joined the Agency, I saved the ass of an 'arvin' general"—ARVN, Army of the Republic of Vietnam—"during an ambush on the Cambodian border. He never forgot. When he heard I was being assigned to Saigon with the Agency, he picked me up in his helicopter and showed me his family's coconut plantations, including a beautiful little island covered with flowers and fruit trees and palms, all within swimming distance of the Mekong Delta. Had little thatched huts for the grove workers who came over every couple of months to tend the trees. Bali-fucking-Hai, boys. That night, the general brought me two gorgeous virgins and said it was only the beginning, that I could have anything else I wanted."

"Two virgins," Stan said through his drool. "Oh yeah, baby."

I backhanded Stan's shoulder and said, "The island, right, Dutch? It was the island you wanted."

"No, you're both right. I wanted the island and the virgins. The general said, 'Sure, anytime, you just let me know.' When I told the Three Stooges about the offer, their faces looked just like yours—kids peering into a candy shop. Yummy-yummy in the tummy.

"Curly says, 'Five ladies for each man. Your general handles procurement, gives us the twenty girls' names. We each draw five.' Curly actually did have a shaved head, only he wasn't fat and always carried a Swedish K submachine gun. One mean motherfucker.

"Then Moe, the smart one, says, 'Rules, we've got to have some rules.' All of us looked at him. He rubbed his chin, like he was some Roman emperor, and said, 'Golden Rule Number One: No sloppy seconds.' We clanked our beer mugs together and took a long draught. 'And Golden Rule Number Two: No more than one exposed Johnson in any one room.'

Another toast followed by very loud cowboy calls that nearly got us thrown out of the bar."

"Excellent rules," Stan said. "I wish I had a pen and paper."

"I think we can remember them," I said. "Go on, Dutch."

"The general sent his workers to the island and got it all prettied up for us," he continued. "Then he brought me to his big house in Saigon one night and paraded in twenty of the finest young women I'd ever seen. Fact is I've never seen better since. He says, 'If any fail to meet your standards, Sergeant, I will replace them immediately.' So after I get my eyes back in my head, I say, 'These'll do just fine, General.'

"Very next two-week break from duty, we go out to the island on a sampan and find those twenty fillies waiting for us, ready and willing to experiment for the first time with their womanhood. We want to oblige them right away, but then Larry, the quiet one, the one everyone forgets is around, says: 'After we divide them up, boys, we got to find a way to tell them apart. If we don't, believe you me, we'll be making mistakes and double-dipping and cutting one another's throats over them.' Larry didn't say much, but when he did, we all listened.

"Larry doffed his issue beret and said, 'As agreed, we put the names in here, each draw five, then each choose a color. The girls in your group have to wear armbands in the color you choose. No confusion, no accidents, no confrontations, no problems.'

"It was a fantastic plan. I was green. Before that day, my favorite color was blue, but now it's green, always will be. I want my fucking corpse wrapped in green velvet for burial.

"Our ladies were never in waiting, right up to the end of the war. We were kings, goddamned kings."

Stan and I were mesmerized by this story. Sitting on the tarmac in lawn chairs on that steamy southern Virginia summer day, we decided, without exchanging a word of consultation, that together we would one day find an island and on it establish our own colony of carousal.

"Larry caught a round six months after we settled the island," Dutch whispered. "He died on the chopper ride back to a field hospital. His five girls were redistributed by lottery. I got two stunning beauties. To this day I can remember all seven of my girls' names, each one like the call of a songbird. But shit, no matter how hard I try, I can't fucking remember Larry's real name. How the hell does a man forget something so goddamned important?"

After that melancholy reverie, Dutch perked up again, and he told Stan and me that, on the island, he'd never been happier in his life, his every whimsical need and desire attended, his every dream fulfilled. To this day, he confided, when he was feeling down, he simply closed his eyes and let his mind drift back to the island, where for two years he had been a king.

# 5

# SPARTA

5 June 1993.

Two kings ruled the ancient city-state of Sparta. Much of the regime's day-to-day governing, however, fell to its elders and overseers.

On our Sparta, Stan and I were, of course, the kings. The two oldest women became our Council of Elders, which made them effectively our advisors and assistants. The remaining three ladies, all younger, divided the island's administrative duties, serving as our Overseers. Unlike its namesake, our Sparta did not worship self-denial.

The second *tranche* of five women—all, by design, slightly younger and less educated than the first— willingly assumed the role as the island's working class, though Sparta demanded no actual labor of note. Stan's early pension and a piece of my life savings were put to good use in that regard, leaving everyone with ample time to pursue leisure activities.

To avoid confusion and conflict, all of the girls wore either a green or yellow armband. I was green, just like Dutch.

Our Sparta was a previously uninhabited island in the Cuyo Group, a small archipelago in the far north-ern Sulu Sea of the Philippines, halfway between

Palawan and Panay Islands. We signed a fifty-year lease
for the island, after obtaining approval from the
national and provincial governments. As part of the
deal, we constructed a housing compound and
installed basic plumbing and electrical services (courtesy of a wind-powered turbine, solar panels, and a
diesel generator)—all of which would be turned over
to the Cuyo Islands Fishermen's Federation upon
expiration of the lease.

Before we arrived, Sparta was officially unnamed,
though after questioning several natives of nearby
Agutaya Island, we ascertained that the local fishermen called it "Pawikan," which one of the girls translated as Sea Turtle.

"Sparta," Imelda said to me, spitting out the word,
wrinkling her nose. "Not a pretty name. Pawikan is
much better."

Imelda, one of Sparta's Elders, was my favorite
green-armband girl, a top Ateneo University graduate
who'd always been relegated, by her country's frail
economy and vulgar chauvinism, to lowly sales posi-
tions. In Manila, using my skills of persuasion, honed
by years of enticing reluctant traitors, I'd swept Imelda
off her feet, away from a dead-end job, and into my
harem, where her passions were unleashed, no longer
stifled by her culture's fickle mores.

"But Sparta has grand meaning," I explained.

"Not to us," she said, flinging an arm back toward
the compound to indicate her new sisters.

From that day forward, all of the girls, chattering
constantly in Tagalog, Ilocano, Cebuano, Ilongo, and
Waray-Waray, referred to the island only by its native
moniker.

*   *   *

Stan and I maintained our memberships with the Embassy Club and Commissary in Manila and were thus able to keep the island well stocked with good books, recordings of classical music, gourmet food, and cases of fine red wine. Spartan citizens one and all, regardless of formal education, had an appreciation for the better things in life. Our little society was *not* just about chasing tail; it was also about indulging in genteel pursuits during those rare times when its citizens were too spent to chase tail.

*   *   *

11 September 1994.

Fifteen months after the founding of Sparta, I received orders transferring me to Rome. When I announced the news to my fellow willing castaways, their eyes at once welled up with tears.

"I'll return soon," I told my five girls, lined up shoulder to shoulder on the beach, "when I can no longer resist the call of paradise." Then to Stan, in his wheelchair at my side: "Take care of yourself, amigo."

I was leaving my friend in the capable hands of Irene, Sparta's other Elder. In her previous life, Irene had been an underpaid, undervalued, but highly qualified nurse—a woman of great compassion, wisdom, humility, and devotion. After a string of disastrous affairs with married doctors, Irene had been eager to run away to an island paradise with a silver-tongued gringo, to the promise of a new life unbound by expectations.

Irene's heart had swelled with affection, I think, the first time she saw Stan. With a deep sigh, still gazing at Stan, she'd volunteered on the spot to oversee his medical care.

Always patient and accepting, Irene had never once evinced symptoms of jealousy, even when other yellow-arm-banded girls had come knocking on Stan's door. Knock they did and often, but in the end, Irene got exactly what she'd been waiting for—sole claim on my friend's heart.

"Keep Stan healthy and happy," I told Irene when we were alone on Sparta's jetty. "If anything happens, use the radio-phone and call Makati Medical first, the Embassy second, and then me. Don't worry about false alarms; always err on the side of caution."

Irene put her long, slender fingers on my cheek. Her hand was warm and dry. "I love him very much, you know."

In her simple statement I found the answer to all of my concerns. I took her hand from my face and kissed it. "I know."

"He's getting better every day. Very soon, I think, we'll begin trying."

I raised my eyebrows, soliciting details I already knew.

"A baby—your godchild. A little more therapy and Stan will be ready, so the doctors say."

I gave Irene's hand a squeeze. "Is that what *he* wants?"

She smiled at me, pity in her expression. "Since his brush with death, Stan longs to live outside and beyond his fragile body. My womb can give him what he wants." She looked away from me, unconsciously touching her stomach. "You're a man with dangerous ambitions, Hank. I see that in your eyes. I hope one day you'll embrace love and the miracle of life it promises us."

Irene may have spoken the truth, but at that moment, I couldn't conceive of bringing an innocent child into this pernicious world.

\*   \*   \*

12 September 1994.

Sitting in my outbound plane as it taxied across the tarmac in Manila, I realized that ruling on Sparta, like changing the course of world history, was my destiny. I left the Philippines recharged, ready to return to the grisly but satisfying business of eradicating evil, not only for the good citizens of the world, but also for the sinless child whom Stan would soon sire.

# 6

# GUILLOTINE

Sparta circa April 1994—a flashback.

"That author did his research at Santo Tomas," Imelda said, craning her neck to read the title of my book, a bestseller in Manila about Filipinos who collaborated with the Japanese during World War Two. She added, "UST library has a special section on the occupation."

"The University of Santo Tomas," I stated, recalling what I'd read, "converted by the Japanese into a POW camp, infamous for torture and starvation of prisoners." I closed the book and, raising one eyebrow, gazed over at Imelda. "I didn't know you were such a history buff, young lady."

Imelda drew up her knees, hugging them under her chin. "In 1943, a Japanese major named Kobayashi was appointed administrator of Cavite, just south of Manila. His first week on the job, Kobayashi had his men round up the prettiest girls in the province. My grandmother was one of them. She was only sixteen years old when Kobayashi and another officer took turns with her. But she was lucky."

"Lucky?" I sputtered.

"Kobayashi's men usually killed the girls afterwards, then burned their bodies. And the younger

41

girls, they were often too small for the men, so Kobayashi showed how to cut them open, to make it all easier. Something he learned in China, I heard. Those girls, the little ones, if they weren't killed, usually died from blood loss or infection."

My stomach was churning, threatening to jettison my fruit-smoothie breakfast. "What about your grandmother?"

"She was beautiful, the Cavite festival princess every year. Kobayashi was fond of her, so he let her live. He had many other girls, but she was his favorite—he always came back for my grandmother. She was lucky to have survived."

★   ★   ★

Circa May 1994.

Spurred into action by this ghastly story, I visited Santo Tomas a few weeks after my return to Manila. As Imelda had said, the school's library held hundreds of books on Japan's occupation of the Philippines, and several volumes mentioned Major Takashi Kobayashi, described by one writer as "the bestial Japanese overlord of Cavite Province."

Following a trail of footnotes and bibliographies, I ventured back to the opening days of World War Two, to Japan's bloody march on Mainland China. At the gates of Nanking, Kobayashi—then a junior captain—lost one of his men to the city's weak, scattered defenses. Enraged by this single casualty, the captain commanded his unit to storm the gate and slay every man and boy his troops descried within. Soon, gutters ran red with the blood of Kobayashi's first victims.

After the fall of Nanking, Kobayashi encouraged his men to indulge completely in the spoils of war: to filch whatever caught the eye and to rape the city's every female, young and old alike. Nothing and no one was to be spared.

And then I found historical proof of Imelda's story: The practice of slicing open young girls' perinea, enabling soldiers to ravish even the smallest victims with ease, was developed in a sector of Nanking controlled by one "Captain Kobayashi, T."

Bathed in sweat, I rose from my cubby, dashed to the bathroom, and splashed cold water on my face.

"You all right, sir?" a young library attendant asked. He must have seen I was shaken and followed me in.

"Fine," I answered. "Still getting used to the heat."

Returning to my stack of books, I learned that this same "Kobayashi, T.," using an heirloom samurai sword, had established the all-time Japanese Army record for beheadings. By the war's end, three hundred fifty-two Nanking residents, ninety-nine American prisoners of war, and thirty Filipino guerillas had perished by Kobayashi's blade.

As a testament to sidesplitting Japanese Army humor, Kobayashi became known in the ranks as The Guillotine. His mother and father, I thought, must have been so proud.

Official documents indicated that the Japanese Army *was* proud of Kobayashi, for he was awarded three medals for his "valor" in Nanking and two commendations for his service in the Philippines. Then in early 1943, about the time Kobayashi began his rampage in Cavite, he was honored with a promotion to major.

After the war, U.S. Army General Douglas Macarthur, the Supreme Commander of Allied Forces in the Pacific, rescued countless Japanese war criminals from the rope, especially those like Major Kobayashi, who hailed from wealthy and influential families. They would be the glue, Macarthur had argued, that would bind together a crumbling Japan; these were the capable men who would rebuild the war-torn country.

But *someone* had to answer for those heinous offenses, so a U.S. military court, enjoined by the Supreme Commander himself, brought to trial the Japanese general who'd planned and rendered the attack on Nanking. After enduring a week-long pageant of American justice, the general was convicted, sentenced, and hanged for his "conduct unforgivably far beyond the pale," to quote one wordy document from the tribunal.

(Japanese military communiqués, however, place the general in a field hospital during the "Rape of Nanking." After recovering from severe influenza, he returned to the ravaged city. Shocked and outraged, he commanded his junior officers—among them "Captain Kobayashi, T."—to cease all spoiling activities. The underlings officially acknowledged the order, but after only a brief hiatus, they resumed, though charily, their conduct of atrocities.)

With the general's execution, the Americans closed the case on Nanking and never once inquired about Kobayashi's service record. But The Guillotine was not forgotten: One of Macarthur's senior aides soon found the major a fine civilian job—as manager of a radio factory in Osaka.

Fifteen years later, after moving up steadily through the ranks, Kobayashi became the firm's chief executive officer. In another five years, under the old major's watchful eye, the company, exploiting America's solid-state technology, grew at an unprecedented rate. Then, by the middle 1970s, Kobayashi had grasped the helm of the second largest circuit manufacturer in Japan.

And here the literary chronicle of Kobayashi ended.

I picked up the scent again on the Internet, thanks to several Chinese nonprofit organizations dedicated to the documentation of Japanese war crimes. For years these groups had tried in vain to secure from the Japanese government a full admission of the country's wartime misdeeds.

One of the Chinese nonprofits devoted a full Webpage to "The Guillotine," who in 1990, still spry at the age of eighty, turned over control of the sprawling company to his eldest son, then retreated into a quiet retirement in the mystical city of Kyoto. There, in the home of his vaunted samurai ancestors, he reportedly enjoyed a serene life—meditating, gardening, and playing with his grandchildren.

At the bottom of the page, I found Major Kobayashi's residential address, a blurry shot of his modest but impeccable house front, and a sharp portrait—complete with autograph—of the killer himself, probably posed for a company prospectus.

Wetting my lips, I stared at Kobayashi's picture: thick silver-gray hair, oiled and perfectly groomed; ramrod-straight posture; smooth face, a liver spot on his right cheek; bushy black eyebrows; and those eyes—piercing ebony irises under heavy epicanthic folds.

It was, to me, the image of evil incarnate.

⋆   ⋆   ⋆

12 September 1994.

En route to Rome, I stopped over in Japan, ostensibly for three days of sightseeing. I followed the bilingual signs in Narita International Airport through immigration and customs to a ticket counter, where I purchased a J-Rail pass. I then boarded the airport shuttle to Tokyo. At the city's main terminal, I transferred to a bullet train bound for Kyoto.

I vowed to travel during my stay only by mass transit or on foot, avoiding traceable transport, such as rental cars and taxis.

⋆   ⋆   ⋆

13 September 1994.

After walking for two hours from my hotel in downtown Kyoto to Kobayashi's home, getting lost five times along the way, I settled into a playground swing. From my perch on a terrace above the neighborhood's rooftops, I commanded an unobstructed view of Kobayashi's backyard.

Children soon began frolicking around me, but at a safe distance, caution winning out over curiosity. Then an adorable little girl took a few hesitant steps toward me, the alien, and stood staring at the multitude of sun-lit blonde hairs on my forearms. Would Kobayashi, I wondered, feel an urge to molest and mutilate this innocent child? Perhaps not, I concluded: She was, after all, of his pure and superior race, not some lesser mongrel from China, the Philippines, or America; he bore no record of perversion in his own country.

I smiled at the girl, then resumed my surveillance of Kobayashi's residence. Within twenty minutes I was honored with the old major's presence. Bitter irony—he began practicing *Chinese* Tai Chi Chuan. Where, I wondered, had he learned those gentle longevity exercises? Were they a remnant of his stint in subjugated China? Regardless, he was about to learn that he was laboring in vain.

A flicker of movement at the front of Kobayashi's home drew my attention from the old murderer's constitutional. An attractive gray-haired woman and a younger female—the latter having a striking resemblance to Kobayashi—appeared on the stoop, a porcelain-faced toddler in tow, and headed toward the family mini-van. A middle-age man wearing a white chef's uniform flew from the house and helped the ladies and child into the back of the vehicle. The man, probably Kobayashi's manservant, then hopped into the driver's seat, conveyed the ladies and child down the hill, and merged onto a busier street, turning in the general direction of Kyoto's business district.

Was Kobayashi now alone? I sprinted though the playground, bounded down a staircase to the street, and followed the steeply declining sidewalk to The Guillotine's lair. I rang the bell for the better part of a minute before the elegant, silver-maned master of the house threw open the door.

He stared at me, mouth agape, then said, "May I help you?"

His good English surprised me. None of my research had suggested his fluency in another language.

My jaw too had dropped, so I winched it up and replied, "Uh, yes. Yes you can. So glad to find someone who speaks English. I'm looking for a playground in this area, where I'm supposed to meet my girl-friend. She's a student from my language school." (I knew that Japan's abundant English schools were often staffed with anglophone foreigners.)

Kobayashi's face crinkled into a charming smile. He exuded warmth, affability. I studied him more closely: His sparkling eyes bore no evidence of the odious roles he'd played five decades before. What I'd read and what I was seeing were incongruous, confus-ing. Were my instincts betraying me?

Pointing up the street, Kobayashi said, "The park is there, just up the hill. You'll notice stone steps on your right. Those lead to the playground area."

"Thank you," I said. And then, for some reason, I bowed—deeply. To this day, I don't understand why I did that.

# 7

# SAMURAI

In Manila, shortly before my departure, I had rented a videotape copy of a 1960s-vintage film about the French resistance movement of World War Two. My discovery of the movie at the commissary had evoked in me a strong sentimentality: My father and I had watched the picture together in the early 1970s on broadcast television.

About halfway through the film, a courageous French guerilla slips onto a bridge on an ink-black night and silently strangles two German Army guards.

"What was that?" I remembered asking my father.

"A garrote," he had answered. "Made from piano wire. Sharp as a razorblade." My father, a decorated U.S. Marine Corps veteran of the vicious Korean Conflict, had witnessed all manner of killing.

This time, as I watched the scene alone, the garrote appeared to me as a glowing oracle.

\* \* \*

14 September 1994.

Back in my hotel room in Kyoto, I unstitched a thin wire from the lining of one of my suitcases. Then I disassembled my bath brush and broke the wooden handle in half where I'd scored it with a saw in Manila. I'd also drilled a small hole through the center of each section of brush handle, and into each hole I threaded and lashed an end of the wire.

Now my weapon was complete: a length of sharp, strong wire strung between two handles. It was the oracle realized.

I walked back to the park overlooking Kobayashi's backyard. Right on schedule, the old major appeared and began his slow, deliberate Chinese dance. And just like the day before, the manservant escorted grandmother, daughter, and grandchild to the van and whisked them down the hill and out of sight.

I should mention that I was in light disguise, as I had been on my previous visit: dark brown temporary-color mousse in my sandy hair and five-day growth of beard; tinted round spectacles on my nose, obscuring my pale blue eyes; and oversized clothes, purchased at a flea market in Manila, draped over my angular frame, making me appear stoop-shouldered and gaunt. This was the awkward young foreigner whom neighbors had seen in the park, whom Kobayashi had greeted at his front door. For the second time in as many days, I had slipped into the toilet at a nearby train station, emerging moments later transformed into this harmless bohemian.

I opened a checkered cloth on the park's grass and laid out a picnic for two, as if I were expecting a prospect for romance. This prompted smiles from several of the middle-aged wives, wedged into their dismal ruts of cooking and childcare, who were minding their sons and daughters at play.

An hour and a half later, once again on schedule, the van returned Kobayashi's lineage to their home.

More than enough time for an assassination, I calculated.

I assumed the role of a crestfallen young man, having been stood up by my date. As I slowly gathered my things, a woman in her middle thirties gazed at me with sad, sympathetic eyes, tilted her head to the side, and shrugged. I smiled at her and nodded—Yes, my gesture implied, there are more fish in the sea.

\* \* \*

15 September 1994.

On my third and last day in Japan, I stuffed my English teacher's garb into my backpack, at the bottom of which was my coiled garrote. I checked out of my hotel and secured my other luggage behind the front desk.

I again trudged over to Kobayashi's home, stopping along the way for the routine identity change. Climbing the last hill, I glanced at my watch. According to my previous observations, the van should have already departed. I glanced up in time to see the vehicle flash by, catching a glimpse in one of the van's rear windows of a small pale face under a mop of black hair.

I strode up Kobayashi's walkway and rang the doorbell until the old major appeared. He stood at the threshold, scrutinizing me, eyes narrowed, then his face softened.

"Did you find the park?" he said.

"Your directions were perfect. But I'm lost again. I'm supposed to meet my girlfriend today at a shrine—I've been walking around for an hour and can't find it. Sorry to bother you again."

He waved his hand, dismissing my concern.

I pulled a tourist map from my pocket and fumbled it open. "The name sounds something like 'shogun,' or maybe 'shodun.'"

"If you're looking for the Shoden-ji temple, you're definitely lost. It's at least a twenty-minute walk from here." Helpful Kobayashi reached out and took the edge of my map, and I angled it toward him so that he could read. He squinted, old eyes in need of refraction.

In a flash I grabbed his extended right arm and twisted it clockwise, simultaneously pressing the palm of his hand back toward his inner forearm. While the fluttering map was still in midair, I used my other hand to lock out his elbow and push him into the house. I kicked the door closed and guided the war criminal into his neat, spare, well-varnished home.

In the middle of the living room, I tapped the back of Kobayashi's knee with my foot, coaxing him face-down onto a tatami mat. I said, "If you struggle, I will break your arms and legs. If you cry out, I will crush your voice box."

"I will not resist," he said in a remarkably composed voice.

I released him and stepped back. He took his time rolling over—he was in his mid-eighties, after all. He slowly levered himself up into a cross-legged sitting position on the mat. He hung his head, staring down at his lap. I remained standing, ready to leap forward and make good on my bone-smashing, throat-gouging promise.

"Do as you must," he finally said, still not looking up.

"What does that mean?"

He took a deep breath. "You are not a petty thief. I'm old, but not blind. You are here for something other than robbery."

"You are indeed not blind."

A minute, maybe more, passed without a word being exchanged between us. Kobayashi's retirement home was cool, quiet, tranquil—just as a tomb should be, I thought.

"I robbed myself," he said at last, "of peaceful domesticity, of a man's ultimate satisfaction that only comes at the conclusion of a full and moral life. Such a fulfilled man has great fortune, for he can look upon his children and grandchildren with clear and appreciative eyes. Then he can surrender to the simple enlightenment of old age, finally comprehending the unconditional love that comes so naturally with unspoiled youth, with its almost infinite capacity for authentic affection and kindness."

The old murderer certainly had charm and charisma, not to mention an astonishing command of my native tongue. "Where did you learn English?"

"Private tutors...like you." He let out a nervous chuckle. "I recognized early in my life that English was the language of commerce, and thus of profit."

"You were lucky to enjoy such bountiful earnings." I slid my hand into my pants pocket and felt the reassuring shape of my garrote. "You mentioned that you robbed yourself of a peaceful domesticity. Truth is, you robbed hundreds, perhaps thousands, of that and so much more."

A tear fell from the old man's eyes onto the tatami mat. I couldn't believe it. He was either genuinely remorseful or one hell of an actor.

"When the U.S. Army released me," he said, "I thought I'd escaped retribution for my crimes, my excesses, my pleasures, my twisted view of humanity. But they had unknowingly sentenced me to a lifetime of horror in which I saw forever my own children and later my grandchildren raped and beheaded in my nightmares."

"At least you had dreams, be they good or bad. At least you were able to know your children, to watch them grow to adulthood, and then to lift their children onto your knee. I've even seen your grandson, being raised in the comfort and privilege you've created for your family."

For the first time his head jerked up. He gawked at me, mouth hanging open, panic in his eyes.

"Not my style, Major. I don't subscribe to the methods of the Japanese Army. I'll give your family the chance you denied so many others."

His face relaxed, and then he seemed to fold in on himself, to shrink. The vigorous old soldier and business executive seemed suddenly frail, pitiful.

His head again sank, and he spoke down at the tatami mat: "Everything you say is true, indisputable. So many times I've wanted a courageous man to come and take my life, to tear me from my cowardice. I've yearned to be tormented, mutilated, to have a small sample of my own incomprehensible crimes visited upon me with great prejudice and without mercy. This torture I so crave would not absolve me, it would not relieve me of any guilt, but it would be perfect justice. My shame would finally be exposed and given rightly to my heirs, who would bear my burden for eternity, generation after generation."

I pulled two pieces of paper from my coat pocket and unfolded and smoothed them on the mat in front of Kobayashi. "These should properly expose your shame—one for your family and one for me, to be mailed to a war-crimes organization for wide dissemination." I had typed the document on my Wang computer in Manila and had printed out two copies.

"I need my reading glasses."

"I'll summarize. This is a conspectus of your worst crimes against humanity, including your routine murders of unarmed and malnourished American prisoners, and Chinese and Filipino citizens. It also describes your role in mass rape and mutilation of women and girls. It is based on my extensive research into your wartime service. You may trust that it is accurate, if not complete. I would've needed a dozen more pages to record the full scope of your crimes."

I tossed my Mont Blanc fountain pen onto Kobayashi's lap. His tears were flowing freely now.

"Don't get the pages wet," I said.

The major wiped his eyes and picked up my pen with a trembling hand. With a Western flourish, probably the result of many international business deals, he signed both copies. The signature matched what I had seen on the Internet. He held out my pen.

"Put it down on the mat and turn your back to me. Stay seated."

He did as ordered and craned his neck, obviously expecting to receive the executioner's blade. "Thank you," he said.

Facing death, the old butcher had finally found some small honor. He had certainly been haunted by his memories his whole life, that I believed. He had signed a full confession, abdicating his hard-earned, glorious retirement, passing on to his family only devastating humiliation. A fitting punishment would be to let Takashi Kobayashi continue to live with this mortifying disgrace.

But I didn't give a shit about fitting punishment. I cared only about justice and righteousness and vengeance. I snapped on a pair of rubber gloves* and looped the garrote over his head. Then I braced my foot in the center of his back and pulled with all of my might. The wire bit into Kobayashi's neck, first meeting resistance at his windpipe.

I was amazed that the old man still sat proudly upright—legs crossed, hands clasped in his lap. I leaned back and pushed with my leg until the wire sliced right through his ancient rice-paper neck, until the weapon snagged again, this time on his cervical vertebrae.

In the end, blood had splattered all around the front of Kobayashi, but none on me, as I had planned and hoped. My weapon had the advantage of requiring attack from behind, where people are most vulnerable, and of keeping the killer shielded from the victim's hemorrhaging.

I very carefully tugged my garrote free and then wandered through the house until I found a bathroom. There, still wearing the rubber gloves, I washed and disassembled my weapon.

I returned to the living room, pocketed one of the confessions along with my pen and said to Kobayashi's inert body, "The gruesome suffering you sought is now being conferred on you by a God in Whom you never believed."

I slipped out of the Kobayashi home, retrieving my tourist map from the porch, and hiked up to the Shoden-ji temple, where I disposed of my garrote and gloves in the licking flames of a prayer fire. As I

---

* Mr. Anlaf noted that his subsequent hits demanded complete surprise, precluding the use of gloves as a forensic precaution.

watched the handles turn to ash and the wire melt into a thin pool, I felt the warm embrace of a thousand wronged souls, thanking me for tipping the scales of justice ever-so-slightly closer to center.

# 8

# PIMP

19 September 1994.

I got off on the wrong foot in Italy and feared that I would be unable to fulfill my internal pledge of returning to my CIA duties with renewed vigor. My Rome Station branch chief had apparently received an informal report on my inconsistent, lackluster performance.

But from the vehemence of his disapproval of me, my new supervisor, I suspected, was concerned less about my uninspired work in Manila and more about my widely rumored debauchery on Sparta. Hallway scuttlebutt, not intelligence, had always been the real lifeblood of the CIA.

"We do things differently here," my new boss said at my in-briefing.

"Different from what?" I asked.

"Manila Station shoots from the hip, like a gunslinger. The game in Europe is more refined, more sophisticated. Old World espionage is a fine art, developed over centuries of practice. No cowboys here."

"Sometimes you have to climb down into the sewers to chase down rats, a fact that knows no geography."

He snorted and jutted out his jaw. "Rats are unpredictable, diseased, more trouble than they're ever worth. We need none of them infecting our exemplary stable of assets."

His fairytale message finally penetrated my thick skull. On occasion I can be awfully slow . This, I realized, was an ideological fencing match that I could not win. I was junior in rank to my opponent and was hamstrung by CIA's Scarlet Letter: a bad reputation.

"No rats in Rome," I said in a cheery tone, "note to self. Time to stay topside, out in the sun with the clergy and tourists."

The branch chief frowned, and one of his eyes twitched. He obviously lacked an appreciation for my humor's sardonic edge.

His name was Tom Murrow, and he was a devout Mormon. The Agency always recruited heavily from the Church of Latter Day Saints. It made good sense: LDS adherents were often bilingual from two years of overseas missionary work, were less likely to have indulged in the use of illicit drugs, and often sailed right through the CIA's background investigation and polygraph examination. The latter, by the way, posed an insurmountable obstacle to many an otherwise qualified candidate.

Over the years, I had the privilege of working with many CIA officers who happened to be Mormon, and I found the lion's share of them to be solid and trustworthy. But Tom, like fanatics of other faiths, constantly confused professional honor and ethics with his private system of belief and morality, and judged harshly any colleague who was found lacking by his hallowed standards.

Tom's zealotry had led him to ignore blatantly the time-tested rules of the world's second oldest profession, which, despite his protests, shared many techniques with the first. He was under the ridiculous misconception that an intelligence officer could recruit spies without first identifying and then preying upon the target's weaknesses and venalities, most of which were one and the same. In Tom's fantasy world, an intelligence officer was a do-gooder who skipped into a room and simply enlisted those people who were naturally predisposed to the United States and its ventures.

But in the real world, my grimy world, an intelligence officer strove to form a relationship with *any* target—the good, the bad, and the ugly alike—as long as they had demonstrable access to people or things of interest to the U.S. Government. Officers typically founded such relationships on actual or contrived "commonalties," which for many predisposed to treachery were only the most sordid pursuits, and then maneuvered the target into a position wherein he or she could be suborned into committing espionage.

You get the idea: My new supervisor and I held fundamentally different ideas on how our job should be, and could be, done. I was nursing the Mother of All Migraines by the end of our first encounter.

★ ★ ★

My standard response to looming conflict was either to disengage completely or to stand my ground and fight—and by fight I mean that I would literally take up fisticuffs with my antagonist. Even back in high school, long before my formal training in martial arts, I earned a reputation as a scrapper, as a boy who, if pushed too far, would leap at a bully's throat.

No matter how many injuries I sustained in the process, I continued to inflict damage with wild abandon. I discovered early on that very few big men would risk disfigurement just to claim small bragging rights for having won a contest against a smaller opponent.

In Tom's case, though, I couldn't very well pluck the eyes from his skull or reduce his gonads to a dangling sack of crushed chickpeas. That would only get me sent home and possibly prosecuted. Besides, I needed to stay put. I'd already identified my next assassination target, and Rome was the perfect kickoff point for this mission.

So, following my established pattern of behavior, I exercised Option Number One and made myself scarce by walking the streets of Rome for hour upon hour. In the espionage profession, we are trained to familiarize ourselves intimately with our area of operations, to look for suitable signal sites, meeting locales, and hotspots—things to be avoided like police stations and security cameras. In CIA jargon, this activity is called "casing."

Under the guise of energetic casing, I escaped protracted contact with—and thus any reproach from—Tom, or "Santo Tommaso," as he became known among us working stiffs.

\* \* \*

4 October 1994.

Though I planned to kill next in North Africa, the hand of Fate haled me instead down a dark street in Rome, where I stumbled upon a scoundrel and his innocent victim.

She was a gypsy, I later learned, wrested from her mother's battered arms and forced to work off a staggering family debt. Her father, desperate to save his only child, surrendered to the three Mafiosi a tangle of cheap jewelry, the sad total of his vagabond estate. But the gangsters swatted the baubles aside, beat the old couple senseless, and then dragged the daughter away, sniggering with ill intent.

A month later, at night, as I strolled near Rome's ancient Diocletian Baths, the foul outcome of this misdeed emerged from the gloom like a wraith. The gypsy, pale and gaunt, lingered alone on a shadowy corner, wearing knee socks and penny loafers, a pleated navy miniskirt, a skintight button-down blouse, and a red beret—obviously a prostitute, adorned to attract those with certain warped proclivities.

Normally, I would've averted my eyes and swerved to the far edge of the sidewalk, communicating my disinterest in the girl's services. But her huge, dark, sad eyes captured my gaze, begging, pleading for my approach. I took a closer look at her: small heart-shaped face, full lips, cropped black hair, tiny protruding ears, spindly arms and legs. Standing on the corner, she moved not a muscle, feet together, shoulders slumped, arms dangling by her sides.

The girl had a sweet, elfin beauty to her, which set her apart from all of the other painted trollops I'd seen walking Rome's streets. This incongruity awakened the field operative in me, heightened my senses, and within a matter of seconds I located the man tucked into the alley behind her, his face a lumpy silhouette.

The girl, noticing where I'd glanced, shut her eyes and drew in a deep breath.

I fell into character, which comes as second nature to experienced spies, and which in this case was that of a lonely, lustful young man. I slowed to a stop and leered at the advertised flesh, ogled her from head to toe, pausing predictably at her upturned breasts and long, slender legs. I formed my mouth into a lascivious grin, raised my eyebrows, and sauntered over to her.

"May I buy you a glass of wine?" I said in Italian, opening the negotiations.

Right on cue, the man from the alley glided over. In a rough Neapolitan accent he said, "You find my cousin attractive?"

"I and millions of other men."

He cackled, emitting a vapor of distilled spirits, and leaned toward me into a shaft of light from a nearby street lamp. His boxer's nose was a zigzagging tribute to San Francisco's Lombard Street, his cheeks and brow were crosshatched with fine scars, and the top of his right ear resembled the cogs of a bicycle sprocket. He was a good two inches shorter than I, but probably outweighed me by twenty or thirty pounds.

"My cousin and I," the pimp said, nodding at the girl, "we're on our way to borrow some money for a family emergency. But if you could loan me three hundred thousand lira"—almost two hundred dollars—"she would be free to...to share a bottle of wine with you."

I glanced over at the girl. She was staring off into the darkness, her eyes moist, desolate.

"Small price to pay," I said, turning back to the pimp, "for the honor of enjoying the company of such a beautiful woman."

Another cackle, followed by more liquor fumes. "You're German? A businessman?"

A reasonable supposition on his part: My Italian was at best mediocre, and I was well dressed, having begun my walk earlier in the day from the embassy.

"Belgian," I answered, "attending a medical convention."

The pimp flashed a picket-fence smile, a proud trophy, no doubt, of his many skirmishes. He was likely thinking that a wealthy physician would not bother with haggling and would settle for the opening bid.

Confident of his sale, the pimp became more direct: "This one"—cocking his head toward the girl—"she's fresh, her first night on the streets. But no prude, we've made certain of that, trained her well for the past month." He scratched his crotch. "She'll do what you want, *anything* you want."

The girl shuddered and rocked from toe to heel. I thought for a moment that she would topple over, but she bit her lip and kept on her feet. Tears broke the dam of a lower eyelid and sluiced down her smooth, olive-toned face.

I needed no more convincing. I rummaged through my topcoat with my left hand, as if searching for my wallet but actually drawing the pimp's attention from my right. Without altering my stance, I lashed out with the heel of my palm, driving it up and into the pimp's nose.

He stumbled away, his head thrown back, his mouth a large oval. He caught his balance, blinked his watery eyes a few times, and then focused on me, a look of incredulity on his face. Several seconds after my attack, his nose finally reacted and flushed out a torrent of blood.

To some, the appearance of one's vital fluid saps them of all will to fight; with the pimp, it had the opposite effect. He wiped his nose with a sleeve, squared off, and closed on me with the measured movements of a seasoned pugilist. I too assumed a fighting position and waited to turn the energy of his attack against him.

But he failed to oblige me. Instead, he shuffled a semicircular course beyond my striking and grappling range. At the end of his circuit, abreast of me on the left, he executed a smart about-face, retraced his path by two or three steps, then darted sideways into my perimeter. In a flash, he fired a left jab at my face, but I had just enough time to bob out of the way. I leaned back in and reached for his arm; I wanted to rive his elbow like a wishbone—payback for his taking a nasty swipe at my teeth. That was when a right hook came out of nowhere and slammed into my temple.

I'd been punched countless times before, but I'd never been hit so hard in my life. The pimp's hook—the second half of a standard combination—flicked me to the ground like a discarded cigarette butt. I could see only fuzzy shapes and shadows, and my cranium felt shattered, a web of fissures on the verge of disintegrating into a pile of puzzle pieces. A wave of nausea came up from my stomach and lodged in my throat. I heard the pimp scraping toward me with his shuffle-step. The girl gasped and said something in Italian that sounded like "Knife." I wasn't sure; a gong was still clanging in my ears.

Then came the signature click of a switchblade, and I knew that I was finished. Dead would be my alter ego Odin, who, now with two acknowledged kills, was at last beginning to receive some notoriety. Odin and I would perish anonymously on the streets of Rome, for a nameless girl forced into prostitution, at the hands of her sadistic pimp. No guns blazing, no valorous last stand.

Without warning, the nausea popped free of my throat and brought out with it a long stream of vomit. As I sat spitting and gagging and thinking of my unde- niable brain damage, my head miraculously cleared. My air passage unobstructed, I drew in one long breath, and the world snapped into sharp focus.

I remained motionless, my head still hanging to one side, and looked askance at my attacker, who had apparently halted his advance while I unburdened myself of a large and colorful spaghetti dinner. I then entered my pitiful plea: "Not my face, please. For my parents' sake."

The pimp wiped his bleeding nose, smirked, and slashed his blade through the air. "Not the face. No, no. Lots of other places to cut."

He took one step closer to me, and I hurled my heavy key ring into his eyes, coming up on a knee as I followed through. (I was a baseball pitcher in high school, threw in the upper eighties with great accura- cy.) The pimp screeched and began blindly brandish- ing his weapon, clutching his gouged eyes with his free hand.

From my crouch, I executed a low sweeping kick, smashing into the pimp's right knee with my heel. The unmistakable cracking noise meant that I had dis- located, perhaps even broken, his kneecap. The pimp came down hard but caught himself on his forearms. He adeptly rolled onto his backside, facing me. My keys had rendered his left socket a red, pulpy mess, but his right eye was clear and angry and locked onto me like a laser sight.

He whipped his arm around, and as he recoiled for another go, I jerked back just beyond his reach. I glanced down at my left shoulder and was shocked to see a clean slice through my topcoat. He'd gotten me. A small stain of blood appeared and quickly grew, saturating a grapefruit-size patch of fabric around the wound.

I sprang to my feet, ripped off my coat, and spun it around my right forearm. The pimp, crippled and partially blind, was yelling at the top of his lungs. From what little I comprehended, he was questioning my ancestry. Wincing and still cursing, he struggled to his feet but was hobbled beyond effective advance or retreat.

I circled him slowly, listening to a mental replay of my jujitsu instructor's lessons, concentrating on my breathing, focusing my mind. Within seconds, I found myself immersed in the tranquility that surrounds a true warrior in combat. The pimp's fate had been ordained; I had only to see the ritual through to its end.

I was now witnessing the scene in slow motion, an amused passenger inside my own body. When the pimp lurched toward me, chopping down with his knife, I darted in, effortlessly, crouched beneath his clumsy attack, and brought up my padded right forearm, blocking him in mid-strike. I pivoted behind him and trapped his hand and weapon against my forearm with my left hand. Maintaining this grip, I swung my left elbow up and over his locked-out arm, my armpit closing over his elbow. I dropped my full weight onto the limb, pressing the pimp face-down toward the sidewalk. In my armpit, I felt his elbow hyperextend and snap. He bellowed like an Italian opera tenor and dropped his blade.

I released my hold and pinned his torso beneath one of my knees. From my shirt pocket, I plucked my

Mont Blanc fountain pen, flipped off its cap, and stabbed it into the pulsing artery on the side of the pimp's neck. I withdrew my makeshift weapon and watched with some amusement as blood spurted from the small hole—a puncture in the side of a full water cooler.

As I wiped clean my field-expedient shank, I cast a pleasant smile over at the girl, who was cowering by the base of the lamppost, her eyes bulging like a lemur's. I then turned back to my handiwork and saw that the pimp had stopped twitching, so I rolled him over and on his forehead drew my mark, for I had left my calling cards in a strongbox at my apartment.

Gazing at my victim's pallid, battle-scarred face, I realized that this killing was a departure for me. I had slain my first two targets in accordance with *lex talionis*, the primal law of direct reprisal, for past atrocities against mankind. But with this hit I was able to stop a villain dead in his tracks, literally, and in so doing to save a precious life from further torment.

# 9

# JIHAD

Ahmed Elliot El-Gamal. Born in Cyprus to an Egyptian architect father and an English noblewoman of withering assets and standing. Educated in private schools in Canada to avoid the racism and criticism of his snobbish kindred in the Isles. Grown into a man in his middle thirties without any claims to tradition, history, or ethnic pride. Abandoned, ridiculed, and disillusioned by his Western lineage.

His Arabic blood roused in him both curiosity and fear. He was a man on a quest for himself, looking desperately for what and who he was and would be. He was a man drawn strongly to his once-forbidden Islamic self, to its unwavering devotion to God, and, alas, even to its worrisome extremism. He was a man in penumbra—uncertain if he should stay in the safety of light or move into the alluring mystery of shadow.

He was a man in search of his genuine identity and a meaningful destiny. But beneath his storm-swept and frustrated exterior, he was both deceitful and devoid of identity.

He was not a real man at all.

★   ★   ★

17 November 1994.

I created Mr. El-Gamal in Rome after reading an article in a prominent British newsmagazine that I admired for its detailed and even-handed reporting. The essay described the then-recent slaughter of Western tourists, mostly Americans, at the ancient city of Luxor. This horror was carried out at the hands of the infamous group known as "The Holy War of the Nile Headwaters," which the U.S. Intelligence Community called the Upper Nile Jihad, or UNJ.

I justified my alias-documentation request for Ahmed Elliot El-Gamal by volunteering to pursue a freelance money-mover and procurement agent, Ali Hassan, a man connected to both Hamas★ and the UNJ. Hassan, a shrewd, dubious, and devout merchant, operated from the island of Cyprus and would only deal with Middle Eastern natives who demonstrated a tendency toward religious extremism. So I proposed that I Arabize myself, assuming the mixed-blood identity of El-Gamal.

Despite Tom's grumbling, Headquarters approved my request and worked up a beautiful set of Cypriot and British alias documents, complete with passports. Another query to Headquarters brought me a pair of tinted contact lenses and more temporary hair dye mousse, the same brand that I used when I dispatched Kobayashi to his Final Judgment. My con-

---

★ Harakat al-Muqawamah al-Islamiyya, or Islamic Resistance Movement, which carries out terrorist operations against Israel from the Gaza Strip and West Bank. The group is referred to interchangeably as HAMAS, the acronym of its full name, and Hamas, the Arabic word for "courage."

tribution to the El-Gamal persona comprised my basking every weekend in the sun of the Amalfi Coast, bronzing my skin.

A sizeable portion of my monthly operational voucher consisted of claims for dark tanning oil. Being in the clandestine service of one's country occasionally had its benefits.

* * *

14 December 1994.

I became very familiar with Cyprus. I first visited the island as Hank Anlaf, American tourist, on a secret reconnoitering mission.

Ahmed Elliot El-Gamal himself followed Hank to the island. Though Ahmed ostensibly spent his youth in Canada and the United Kingdom, he would, I thought, have at least a working knowledge of his birthplace.

El-Gamal soon became comfortable processing through Cypriot immigration and customs. He took quick notice of people with dual citizenship and began to mimic their expert, effective, alternating use of documentation as they moved through the bustling port of entry.

Ahmed eventually secured a six-month lease on a loft on the outskirts of Nicosia, the nation's capital. From this base of operations, he struck out and explored the city, visiting key locations of his legend, making the cover story more memorable.

Observant El-Gamal became a freelance journalist and sold three short travel pieces to local publications. With the ink of this makeshift writer's résumé still wet, he approached a small Cypriot press and held out to the proprietor his proposal for a memoir on the turbulence of a half-breed life. Three hours later, over tar-pit Turkish coffee and under an arthritic overhead fan, the enthusiastic publisher and El-Gamal signed a no-advance contract, the terms of which clearly disadvantaged the aspiring writer.

As if I—I mean Ahmed—cared.

El-Gamal was now ready for my research expedition to the land of his supposed father's birth, to the land of the pharaohs and pyramids. To the sanctuary of the Upper Nile Jihad.

# 10

# WIDOW

19 December 1994.

My pursuit of Ali Hassan granted me admission to a strictly compartmentalized CIA database for Hamas and UNJ reporting. I spent many hours in front of my terminal, stalking my prey.

In Luxor, the UNJ terrorists had sprayed both sides of the tourist bus with automatic gunfire and had then detonated a remote-controlled bomb adhered to the vehicle's petrol tank. The shaped charge, by design, splashed burning fuel throughout the bus's interior. Most of the passengers were incinerated where they sat, bleeding, debilitated by the initial fusillade. With their clothing ablaze, four people, somehow still ambulatory, attempted to flee the inferno but were cut down by a hail of bullets from the waiting terrorists. In all, twenty-three people were killed, seventeen of whom were Americans.

Other tourists, hiding behind crumbled pieces of the ancient civilization, reported later that they listened to the bloodcurdling screams of the passengers as they burned to death. These corroborated statements also described the terrorists dancing around the bonfire, laughing and cheering and hugging one another, before they rallied their eight-man unit and disappeared into the sands of the desert.

As I read about the merciless funeral pyre, my rage came to a full boil.

★   ★   ★

I lifted nary a finger to rout the UNJ terrorists. The Egyptian Intelligence Service, or EGIS—pronounced "ee-jiss"—in CIA jargon, ran them to ground for me.

According to the cables in my database, EGIS had no information on the whereabouts of the perpetrators. They were stymied. But within a month of my addition to the Hamas and UNJ bigot lists, I received a finished intelligence report, complete with geocoordinates that placed the terrorists at an isolated UNJ safehouse in the desert south of Aswan, near a large oasis.

I analyzed the report, supposedly stripped of its identifying details for source protection. Having authored a few such documents myself, I quickly deduced from the report's cookie-cutter obfuscation that it had come from a unilateral CIA penetration of EGIS, an Egyptian intelligence officer who was selling his organization's secrets to the U.S. Government. This spy revealed to the Agency what the Egyptian government was keeping from us for fear of igniting the tinderbox of anti-Western Islam sitting under its very secular, and thus very unpopular, hindquarters.

A few days later, I discovered that the U.S. government was a co-conspirator in the suppression of this critical intelligence. My own masters were unwilling to act alone on the tactical lead, citing their concern that we would create a backlash of even greater anti-Americanism in the country and would indeed upset the teetering apple cart of our valuable Arab ally. Politics once again reigned supreme over justice.

Disgusted, I went out that very afternoon and bought a top-of-the-line handheld global positioning system.

\*　　\*　　\*

23 December 1994.

I flew to England and received a brush pass from a London Station officer. We used pre-coordinated visual bona fides to identify each other in the appointed public-access stairwell. I wore a red baseball cap turned backwards and carried a tightly rolled magazine in my left hand; she had a white carnation in her lapel and an issue of the salmon-colored *Financial Times* tucked under her left arm.

She was a professional. Her eyes flickered over me and then resumed the dull, forward-looking gaze of a typical commuter. She smoothly transferred the *Financial Times* to her right hand and bumped into me ever-so-slightly as we passed on the steps, covertly slipping the newspaper into my grasp. Not only was my colleague's clandestine tradecraft excellent, but so too was her appearance. I told myself that I'd have to schedule an unofficial stopover in London one of these days.

At the landing, I betrayed a basic protocol of tradecraft—but for a very important reason. I stopped, turned, and gazed up at my fellow officer's shapely bottom as it swayed deliciously on the last two steps.

*    *    *

24 December 1994.

Christmas Eve. I attended morning services at a nondenominational Protestant church in London. That afternoon I stowed my true name documentation in a safety-deposit box at my hotel and assumed the identity of Ahmed Elliot El-Gamal, whose counterfeit papers had been secured inside a fold of the *Financial Times*. Pushing aside the Agency-issued colored temporary mousse, I applied standard brown dye to my hair and to my four days of facial scruff. I used a mascara brush to darken my eyelashes and eyebrows, and I shaved off my blonde arm hairs. I donned the contact lenses and took a taxi to Heathrow, where I caught an Air France flight, via a brief layover in Paris, to Nicosia.

I dropped my bags at the loft and proceeded to a large Saudi-owned bank. I inquired after the island's best *hawaladar*, a type of cash-transfer house indigenous to the Middle East and South Asia, and came away with a list of three reputable institutions.

*    *    *

30 December 1994.

At each of the three *hawaladars*, I remitted one thousand dollars to different pro-Palestinian but legitimate charities. (A CIA crash course had given me a command of rudimentary Arabic, a suitable fluency for my expatriate upbringing.) At each exchange I solicited a recommendation for an individual or organization that could handle more "delicate" transfers to the Occupied Territories. I was coldly turned away at one *hawaladar* but, between the other two, received a total of seven names.

Seven has always been my lucky number, and it was again in the case: Felucca Holdings, Ltd., Hassan's known (to the CIA) cover company, was among them. I now had an overt and provable explanation for how I was led to Ali Hassan and his expertise in unconventional transactions.

I decided that, for this, the actual kickoff of the Hassan targeting operation, I had accomplished enough CIA work to appease the ever-caviling Santo Tommaso. I beat a hasty retreat to my loft and made telephone reservations for a roundtrip flight leaving the following morning. I then enjoyed a home-delivery meal of Greek food and fruity red wine before falling into a luxurious slumber.

*    *    *

5 January 1995.

Upon my arrival in Cairo, I began to dress like an average Egyptian man in a *jallabiya*, a loose-fitting, sleeved robe. I checked into a hotel and sunned myself on its roof and dyed the roots of my growing beard. The city's heat, pollution, and overcrowding were unbearable, so two days later I traveled to Luxor, where I toured the ruins and got a first-hand look at the scene of the horrible crime.

Playing the part of a soul-searching writer, I ventured still farther south to Aswan. My imaginary father, Ahmed El-Gamal Sr., grew up on a farm somewhere south of the city, near a large oasis from which the family had drawn irrigation and potable water for centuries before the construction of Nasser's High Dam. In my broken Arabic, I suggested to anyone who would listen—from hotel clerks to waiters to taxi drivers—that I was bound and determined to scour the desert until I found at least a small trace of my clan's long-abandoned homestead.

Posing as half an Englishman, I expected to face a chilly reception in Aswan, but contrary to my prejudices, every Egyptian with whom I discoursed was indulgent, polite, sympathetic, and very helpful. On my seventh lucky hour in the city, I stopped at a teahouse for a cup of the country's syrupy-sweet brew and a draw on a communal hookah pipe.

Being the only customer at that hour, I easily engaged the elderly proprietress in conversation. She was a widow who ran her late husband's enterprise from behind the scenes, and she seemed to welcome my attention, having probably been ignored by every other male patron for years.

The widow glanced around nervously, searching for any disapproving eyes in the neighborhood, and then settled onto a cushion opposite me. "Those with mixed blood rarely return to Egypt and never, I think, venture beyond Cairo."

(Though I represent the widow's speech as colloquial English, she actually conversed in an Arabic-English pidgin, which I skillfully mimicked in my responses to her.)

She added, "What brings you to Aswan?"

"My father, now dead more than a year. His early childhood was spent on a date farm, some few kilometers south of the city."

"El-Gamal, that's a common name. Where exactly was this farm?"

"My family refused to tell me, but I recall my father once mentioning a large oasis."

The old woman's eyes brightened. "To the south of Aswan is an oasis on the property of the Mohsin family. My ancestral lands are nearby." Her brow furrowed. "But I know not of any El-Gamals from that place."

My prepared cover story was brilliant in its creative ambiguity and unprovable claims. I stared moodily into the depths of my teacup and said, "According to my tight-lipped relatives, the estate was sold sixty years ago, maybe more, when my father was still a small boy. The family moved first to Cairo, then immigrated to Cyprus.

"My father attended university in Lebanon and returned to the island to establish an architectural firm. His success gave the family convenient amnesia about our humble origins. Our history is in constant evolution, staying apace with our growing fortunes. I would not be surprised to learn I'm descended from sharecroppers or even seasonal farm workers, with no place at all to call home."

The sad look on the widow's face and her watery eyes were the equal of applause for my virtuoso performance. I had strummed a veritable concerto on her heartstrings.

"Praise Allah for your honesty and humility," she said, "and may He be with you on your worthy pilgrimage." She sniffled and handed me a skeleton key on a loop of leather. "It's no more than a shack, all that's left of our ancestral homestead, less than two kilometers from the Mohsin oasis. From there you can strike off on walks across the soil that was perhaps once tended by your kinsmen. I pray that Allah will help you find the inspiration for which both your mind and soul so clearly hunger."

As we parted ways, she promised to warn the care-
taker that a pilgrim would be occupying the shack for
a few days. And for the first time since I embarked on
this calling, I experienced a twinge of guilt. Looking
back, I suppose a part of me felt bad for exploiting the
old lady's kindness, perverting her compassion into a
medium for my intended brutality.

The pang was weak, mind you, and produced in
me no lasting qualms or hesitation. I mention it only
for dramatic effect. Truth be told, I was most grateful
for the dowager's unintentional assistance, which
would allow me to reconnoiter and later to launch an
assault against my target without hindrance.

# 11

# CREMATORIUM

6 January 1995.

My GPS locked on to six satellites and calculated a navigational fix that was less than three hundred meters from the reported coordinates for the UNJ safehouse.

I was perched on a rocky, sand-strewn bluff overlooking the isolated dwelling, peering down on it with a compact telescoping monocular, the modern version of a pirate's spyglass. The house, while well maintained, was mysteriously devoid of life. I'd watched it for five straight hours, during which time no one entered or departed.

Finally, a small boy on a bicycle squeaked up, hoisted a big basket that had been lashed to a plywood strip over the bike's rear fender, and wobbled over to the house's front door. After performing an elaborate code of knocking on the jamb, the boy was admitted. The occupants were careful to avoid exposing themselves as the door swung open for a split second.

The boy returned outside within the minute, swinging his now-empty basket in one hand and ogling a pile of shiny coins in his other. This house indeed exhibited a pattern of activity often associated with fugitives, with men on the lam. "Suspiciously vacant" was a term that I'd heard during one of my first CIA operations.

The matching GPS coordinates, the nearby presence of a large oasis, the apparent use of the house as a hideout—these facts would still be insufficient to spur my risk-averse employer to action. But I was not a partner in such institutional poltroonery. I now had more than enough information to conclude that this secluded structure was the refuge of my quarry.

I decided on the spot to attack the very next day, so that I could scurry back to Nicosia and from there back to London and Rome, before the Station—read "Tom"—missed me. But first I had to trail the boy back to his point of origin, where I could subtly elicit from him a few crucial details on the safehouse's inhabitants.

As for my weapon, I had brought with me two garrotes, a primary and a backup, the parts of which I had concealed in the stitching of my luggage and amongst my toiletries. But I was very doubtful that I could separate, surprise, and kill as many as eight trained terrorists with a simple wire. It was then, as I skulked along the ridgeline following the boy, that I began trying to conjure up an alternative, more efficient means to liquidate all of my targets in one fell swoop.

Though I didn't know it at the time, I would soon discover, quite by accident, a most appropriate technique, one that promised a perfect revenge.

★   ★   ★

The boy led me to the bazaar★ of a small village about a mile from the UNJ safehouse. He walked his bike down a narrow alley and leaned it against a chipped adobe wall. Then he sneaked, actually on his tiptoes, through the back door of a cramped native grocery.

From his demeanor, I presumed that the boy was earning some pocket change on the side without his parents' knowledge. To test my hypothesis, I reversed my path, strode in through the shop's front door, and began scrutinizing the myriad stocks of dried beans. With my darkened features and tattered, dusty local clothes, I drew no attention.

I finally spotted the boy, unpacking a box of canned goods and trying to explain to a woman, probably his mother, his brief absence from the store. The boy claimed that he'd been playing soccer with his friends and had lost track of time, but his mother, with her hands on her hips and her face distorted by a scowl, was buying none of it. (Deciphering their simple conversation posed me no great challenge. I had a talent for picking up new languages and was already well on my way to mastering the basics of Arabic.)

Then an inquisitive customer beckoned the woman to the front of the store, giving me a chance to approach the boy. He saw me coming, gave me a hard sidelong look, and then arched his eyebrows, unsure of what to make of this advancing oddity. His puzzlement only grew when I opened my mouth:

"How might a man enlist your private delivery services?"

---

★ Mr. Anlaf opted to use this more familiar term in place of *souk*, the Arabic word for marketplace.

He stared at me, a blank expression on his face.

"Does my peculiar accent require my repeating the question?" I threw a glance toward the front, in the general direction of his mother. "Perhaps much louder?"

The boy's mouth opened into an oval of surprise. Then he pursed his lips, swallowed hard, and said, "We, uh, don't deliver, sir."

"Perhaps I wasn't clear. I perform special *duties* for the Egyptian government and now require your cooperation. Do you now understand what I am saying?"

The boy seemed to take a jolt of electricity. His eyes turned to saucers, his teeth clenched, even his hair appeared to stand on end. Once the initial shock abated, he acknowledged me with a series of spasmodic nods.

From CIA analytical reports, I had learned that many Egyptians became reflexively apprehensive upon mention of the country's infamous police and intelligence apparatuses. I was hoping that the youngster would find me exotic and menacing, would entertain my wild claim as truth, and would thus become suitably distressed. Anxiety and gullibility, I had often observed, were common bedfellows.

"How many men are there?" I demanded.

The boy held up a trembling hand with four fingers extended. I had successfully convinced him of my sinister affiliation.

The terrorists, I noted, were practicing good tradecraft, splitting up into smaller groups. "Any idea where the rest of them are?"

He shook his head and, in so doing, dislodged some tears that had collected in the corners of his eyes.

"We'll have none of that," I said in my best head-master's tone. "Tomorrow, I want you to lend me your bicycle for..." And then I noticed a strange contraption in the corner of the grocery and pointed to it. "What the devil is that?"

After a brief hesitation, the boy shot a hypersonic look toward the object. "For, uh, for water, sir. It rolls."

Another oracle! I had stumbled across the ultimate weapon. I turned back to the boy and glowered at him. "Stay clear of that house, tomorrow and forever. Never go back there again. If you mention this conversation to anyone, you and your entire family will die as the four men soon will, very slowly and very painfully. Any questions?"

The boy shook his head from side to side so violently that I feared for the health of his sloshing brain. As I watched his ferocious wagging, I considered that perhaps this was one poor Muslim boy who would not grow up to kill Americans.

"Remember this," I told the little guttersnipe for good measure, "Muslims, Jews, Christians—we're all Believers in the one true God. None of us deserves to be persecuted for the petty differences between us."

★   ★   ★

I purchased the oracle, stashed it at the widow's shack, and returned to the village. I spent the rest of the day haunting the bazaar, buying all manner of flammable liquids—gasoline, kerosene, lighter fluid, anything that would burn. In the alleyway behind the boy's grocery, I stacked these fuels, each in a different bottle, in a wooden pushcart that I'd found at the shack. The boy, now compromised into my conspira-

cy, kept a close eye on the collection for me throughout the afternoon.

From five separate merchants, I also bought a
dozen lengths of strong chain and as many padlocks.
My last acquisitions were a cigarette lighter and a
black eye-patch. Where hard cash was concerned, I
observed, no one at the bazaar was inclined to ask any
pesky questions.

I paid the boy a handsome fee and struck off
toward the dowager's shack, hauling my incredibly
heavy burden with me. Though the journey was less
than two miles, I toiled with the cart for a solid hour,
arriving bathed in sweat and gasping for air.

I consumed a quick dinner of room-temperature
tea, olives, unleavened bread, and hummus. Thus sustained, I set about the task of filling the oracle's large
plastic barrel. I sealed and tipped over the drum, and
into a socket on each end I fastened one of the handle's two forks.

I'd asked the boy for the name of the contraption,
and he'd provided me an unfamiliar word. Then he'd
hunched his shoulders and danced in a circle. He was
imitating some sort of animal, I supposed, but I could-
n't for the life of me figure it out. I shrugged and
christened the device the "water-roller," a dull but
accurate moniker.

The water-roller was of a simple design: a large
plastic barrel that served as a thick axle between the
two long forks of a metal handle. When fully assembled, the water-roller looked like an oversize manual
lawnmower.

It was an ingenious device, allowing a single person to transport tens of gallons of water to a home or
business with relative ease. Before the advent of the
water-roller, a typical Third World inhabitant was

required to visit a community waterhole several times a day, taking away only what could be carried in one's arms or on one's head.

In this primal context, the water-roller was revolutionary, except that the invention, while donated in the thousands by aid organizations, was finding its way into marketplaces, where it was being sold for a hefty profit. Mine, for example, had cost me a pretty penny even by Western standards.

I tore at my already fraying attire and rubbed some dirt into its fibers. I arranged the patch over one eye and swathed my head and lower face with a filthy turban cloth. I practiced gimping around the shack until I was satisfied with my beggar's gait.

Then I allowed myself a few precious hours of sleep.

★   ★   ★

7 January 1995.

I awoke well before sunrise to the beeping of my wristwatch's alarm. I sprang from my straw-filled mattress and warmed some tea and bread.

After eating, I rushed outside and coiled the chains and locks around the water-roller's handle. I pocketed my two garrotes and the cigarette lighter and, after an initial straining push, established enough momentum to get the roller headed in the right direction—toward the UNJ safehouse. I accomplished all of these tasks while wearing the eye patch, getting used to its feel.

Drawn by the scent of my prey, I covered the intervening mile within twenty-five minutes, despite my heavy load. I stopped and crouched behind a small rise about one hundred and fifty feet from the house's front door. I heard nothing; my cautious, stealthy approach had wakened no one.

I slunk up to the rear of the house, keeping to the pre-dawn shadows. Without a sound, I lashed the backdoor and each of the four windows with chains and padlocks, leaving unsecured only the main entrance. I retreated to my vantage point and waited twenty minutes until the sun broke free of the eastern horizon.

I assumed my hunched posture and pushed the water-roller onto the path. I created as much noise as possible, hoping to dispel any suspicions that I posed any sort of threat.

"You there," I called out in my approximation of a village idiot's grunt, "inside the house. Fresh water, fresh water." I dared not say more, lest they detect my foreigner's twang.

As I struggled to get the roller up the small ramp leading to the porch, I heard scuffling and scraping from inside the house. The tempo of the noises seemed urgent, panicky. Good—I wanted to catch them drowsy and baffled.

I purposefully bumped the roller against the jamb and bellowed, "Fresh water!"

The door cracked open. A single quizzical eye appeared and looked my burden and me up and down. "Wait," the owner of the eye said and slammed shut the door.

Murmuring filtered through the door, followed by the rising tones of a debate. The incomprehensible voices moved a step closer to the door and assumed a calmer tone. The moment of truth was upon me, so I quickly bent over and loosened the filling cap on one end of the barrel. Fuel began spilling out onto the wooden porch.

The door opened again, and this time a different-ly-shaped, angrier eye peered at me. "Who sent you?" The man spat his words at me.

"The boy," I mumbled, "bicycle boy."

I saw the eye relax ever-so-slightly. This was my chance, before he detected the fume-laden air. I took a step back and then pushed forward with all my might, ramming the water-roller through the door. The angry-eyed man was flung to the side and I was inside the house, one large open room from front to back.

I began screaming like a madman, "Water! Water! Water!" and pushing the roller in a wild slalom pattern across the floor, slopping gallons of fuel along the way.

The boy was right: only four men, all dressed in white robes, all with heavy beards. As I smashed through their meager belongings of stacked books, wooden crates, sleeping mats, and lanterns, one of the men yelled, "He's insane!"

And then another: "Stop him! Stop him!"

I swung the roller back around and launched it free into the middle of the room. It crashed into a pile of blankets, spilling forth from underneath a collection of assault rifles, ammunition magazines, and hand grenades.

I gawked at the mess and shouted, "Guns? You have guns?"

The four men were aghast, all focused on their exposed arms cache. The one by the door, still on his knees, said, "C-Cover it!"

The man to my immediate right moved toward the lethal clutter. I pulled taut my garrote and leaped toward him. I lassoed him and wrenched back, pivoting my hips as if I were executing a jujitsu throw. The wire cut halfway through his neck and snapped, sending me stumbling toward the backdoor. I caught my balance and wheeled around. One down, three to go.

The man by the door was on his feet but still doubled over. I must've knocked the air out of him when I battered in. He pointed at me and said, "Kill...him."

I dashed toward the weapons but was intercepted by the man on my left. In his hand was, of all things, a sword, a goddamned scimitar right out of Lawrence of Arabia. He slashed at me two or three times, and I backed away, arms outstretched like a tightrope walker. I glanced over my shoulder and caught a glimpse of the third man, creeping toward me with a shiny silver dagger.

I whipped a vicious backhand toward the knife-wielder and plunged one of my garrote's wooden handles into his trachea. He emitted a guttural cough, dropped his blade, fell to his knees, and clasped his bubbling throat with both hands.

I turned and hurdled over him just as the swordsman hacked at me again. The razor-sharp weapon sliced across my right buttock, and, I must admit, I yelped like an injured puppy.

The swordsman stopped his advance and grinned, amused at my most unmanly exclamation. I had a momentary advantage. I picked up the other man's dagger and hurled it end over end at my attacker. But alas, I was no knife-thrower. It thumped into my assailant's chest, handle-first.

Remember, though, I was once an accomplished baseball pitcher, with a most wicked fastball. The man clutched his chest with his free hand and began clucking like a chicken, trying pitifully to regain a respiratory foothold.

I saw movement out of the corner of my eye and turned to face the man who'd been by the door. He was shuffling across the floor, closing in on the guns and grenades. I sprang toward him, wincing at the pain from my lacerated backside, and we met up as he stooped to retrieve a rifle. I grabbed his extended wrist and twisted so viciously that several bones in his hand and elbow instantly snapped. He wailed like a muezzin calling for prayers.

I wound his shattered arm back and over his shoulder, flipping him forward off his feet. He had no time to catch his fall with his free hand, so his face smashed into the wooden floor. He was out cold, and probably missing some teeth.

I stomped down on the back of his knee, crippling him, and spun around. The swordsman had finally caught up with his elusive breath and was squaring off for an angry bull charge, his weapon cocked back behind his head. I scooped up an assault rifle, worked the action, and hosed him down, full-auto, waist-high. The swordsman folded in two, virtually bisected.

I surveyed the carnage and detected no immediate threats, so I pulled off my turban and wrapped it around my upper thigh, covering most of my gluteal wound and stemming its considerable flow of blood. I recovered the remaining chains and locks and lashed to the water-roller everyone but the man I'd garroted to death. I then bound the roller to the scimitar, which I'd hammered into a tight crack between floorboards. The three shackled men were drifting in and out of consciousness when I picked up the dagger and headed toward the front door. I turned around at the threshold and ignited the lighter.

"For Luxor, boys," I said. "Every good pyre deserves an equally good crematorium in return."

With that, I tossed the flickering lighter into the house.

I limped into the middle of the dusty front yard and stabbed the dagger into an old sandblasted post, tacking up one of Odin's calling cards.

As I hobbled away, I listened to what was, for me, a beautiful symphony—the brass roar of swelling fire and the woodwind howls of final agony.

★   ★   ★

I wore the eye patch all of the way back to the hut before I remembered to take it off.

# 12

## GYPSY

9 January 1995.

In a lavatory stall at Cairo International Airport, I cleaned my wound and dressed it with an antibiotic salve and adhesive bandages. Then I took a handful of analgesics, boarded a plane heading back to Cyprus, and sat favoring my left buttock with an airline pillow wedged under my right.

In Nicosia I transferred to an Air France flight and followed my outbound route home, which included a stopover in London to reverse the brush pass and to dye my hair to its original color. I arrived back in Rome after two full days of travel, wracked with pain.

The gypsy girl, with sympathetic grimacing, skillfully stitched me up, fed me a hot Italian meal, and tucked me into bed. This was the second time that I'd come under her needle, the first being on the night of our meeting, when she mended the pimp's incision on my shoulder.

The girl had been with me for the past three months, ever since our chance encounter on the streets of Rome. I simply couldn't have left her cringing at the crime scene, frozen by shock, so I'd gently helped her up and escorted her to my embassy apartment.

She refused my offer of food for the first day. She curled up in an easy chair and mounted a constant vigil, watching my every move. She flinched whenever I addressed her. Once, as she began to doze off, I approached her with an afghan, and she awoke with a start and recoiled from me. I held out the blanket at arm's length, and she cautiously took it from me. She then gave me a weak smile and blinked away her gathering tears.

I knew at that moment we would soon become friends. I was no longer a threat to her.

She warmed to me during the next week. Her progress was incremental but steady. By our tenth day together, we were having short conversations, and she began telling me in concise chapters the agonizing story of how she happened to fall into the pimp's hands. I felt honored to have played a role in her liberation.

The end of our third week was fast approaching before I asked for her name.

She looked away from me, obviously embarrassed by this glaring omission. "Giuliana Drago," she whispered.

"Have you ever been to a tropical island, Giuliana?"

My dissonant query turned her attention from the awkwardness of our belated, formal introduction. She raised her eyebrows in curiosity.

"In two weeks, I'm going to visit some friends in the Philippines. I'm only comfortable if the balance of my vacation days is hovering just above zero."

Giuliana stared at me, chewing on the morsel I'd fed her. "Who are these friends?" she finally asked.

Her question came wrapped in the chilly tone of prudence, which was understandable after her experiences with vile men. She had every reason to be wary of my oblique offer.

"My *best* friend, actually," I said, "name of Stan Bauer. He's there recovering from a terrible accident."

"All alone?"

I realized that my answer might very well scare her off, that it might lead her to conclude—quite accurately—that I sometimes played a lothario. But as the inscription at CIA Headquarters says, "...[T]he truth shall set you free." Besides, Giuliana had already seen enough double-dealing to last a lifetime.

"Ten women," I said, diving into the ice-cold water, "all rather attractive. And fishermen from a nearby island stop by occasionally to sell rice, vegetables, and the catch of the day." I put on a goofy, disarming grin.

In a most welcome surprise, Giuliana breathed a sigh of relief and visibly relaxed. Then she lowered her drawbridge, inviting me to cross: "An island of women I can handle. Will they accept me?"

"As a sister. How long would you like to stay?"

"Forever," Giuliana answered, without hesitation. "I no longer have a life here. I want to start over." She gazed down and began picking at the afghan, which she had appropriated as her security blanket. "But I have a problem."

"A challenge," I corrected.

"My challenge is I have no passport."

"A birth certificate?"

"With my parents, at a camp outside Perugia." Giuliana picked at the afghan so fiercely that I feared it would unravel. "I cannot face them," she said, "ever again."

"Write them a kind farewell letter and ask for your documents. I will deliver it this weekend. On

Monday, I'll bring the certificate to an acquaintance at the Italian Ministry of Foreign Affairs. You'll have your passport by month's end."

Giuliana looked up at me with an expression of awe. "A challenge," she said.

★   ★   ★

22 January 1995.

Stan was beside himself with happiness. He wouldn't stop shaking my hand.

He peered around me at Giuliana, who was standing fifty feet away, soaking in the many wonders of our tropical paradise. Stan jiggered his eyebrows and said, "See you brought a bottle to the bar."

"She's off limits, to you and me both."

Stan tucked in his chin and squinted at me, disbelief written on his face.

"She's a keeper, Stan, and I refuse to ruin our long-term chances for a few lousy rolls in the hay." I glanced over my shoulder at Giuliana and felt an ache of affection and longing. "Some day, perhaps. If and when the time is right."

Stan smiled and nodded his approval. What his injury had taken from his body it had given to his mind. He was now perceptive, intuitive. He knew exactly what I was trying to say.

"Where's Irene?" I asked.

Stan's face fell slightly, and he answered with a forced levity: "Making the biggest welcome-home dinner you've ever seen, good buddy."

\*     \*     \*

The meal was succulent, an expert mixture of local and imported foods. The Beaujolais Nouveau deserved a standing ovation. The background music, a collection of Mozart violin concertos, was superb. The women were all stunning. Nothing on Sparta had changed.

Three of my five girls were dressed in floral print sarongs, and the other two were in tee shirts and snug denim cutoffs. Everyone was barefoot.

I had earlier introduced Giuliana as the island's newest resident to all of the women. Though I had offered no details of our relationship, current or prospective, I could see on the faces of my green-armband girls that they understood not to come knocking on my door during this visit. Filipinas have a keen instinct for this sort of odd situation and usually respond with astonishing social aplomb and generosity.

Irene busied herself throughout the evening, bringing in the different courses, refilling wineglasses, attending to Stan's every need. She wore a white dress, which fell to her mid-thighs and was secured precariously to her neck by a spaghetti-thin strap. The elasticized garment clung to the amazing roller-coaster curves of Irene's body, which, I observed, bore no evidence of undergarments and appeared to be designed more for exotic dancing than a profession in healthcare. For the duration of the gathering, I concentrated on my plate, my glass, Giuliana, and my five girls, lest Stan notice my gaping at his seductive lady.

After the meal, seven of the girls took Giuliana to a beach to watch the sea turtles struggle ashore to lay their eggs. Two others, according to Irene's schedule, stayed behind to clear the table and wash the dishes. Irene wheeled Stan to their house on the edge of our little compound; he was feeling tired after an exciting day of reunion.

I wandered up to Sparta's highest point, Mount Athena. Stan and I had named the hill after the Greek Goddess of Wisdom—in honor of our island's ten ladies, each bright in her own way. Staring up into the heavens, trying to connect some of the more familiar constellations, I felt a warm dry hand on my forearm.

It was Irene.

In the moonlight I could see the supreme sadness in her eyes. "I saw that look earlier today," I said.

"I was careful to smile during the party."

"Not you—Stan."

Irene gazed down at her feet and wiggled her toes in the grass. She slid her hand down my arm and entwined her fingers in mine.

"I love him so much," she said.

"That should be enough."

Irene kept looking at her feet. "He wants a baby, now more than ever."

"I thought you and he were..." I knew of no tactful way to end the statement.

"His rehabilitation was successful. We tried for months, but nothing has happened. So we flew to Manila last week for medical examinations."

"Are you okay, Irene?"

"It's Stan. His wounds left him impotent."

God was not cutting my friend any breaks. "How's he taking it?"

"The doctor gave me the results and suggested I break the news to Stan." She looked up into my eyes. Tears rolled down her face. She said, "I lied to him, told him he has a low sperm count. I said, with proper diet and rest and exercise, he'd be all right. But I think he knows the truth."

"Maybe the truth is what he needs."

Irene grabbed the sides of my face and pulled me close. "He's fallen into a depression. He stopped his therapy and is becoming weaker. What he needs is a child, Hank. He needs to preserve an unbroken piece of himself. He needs your help."

"What can I possibly do?"

Irene released my face and wiggled out of her white dress. The moonlight drenched her body, tinting her smooth beige skin with a silvery blue. Her figure was flawless, perfect in shape, size, and proportion. She stepped toward me, wrapped her arms around my neck, and again pulled me close.

So that night and every night thereafter I violated the most important of Sparta's Golden Rules, until Irene could give to Stan an heir and, in return, receive from Stan more of his life. More days, weeks, months, years—it didn't matter to Irene as long as it was more.

* * *

4 February 1995.

As always, I took the time in Manila's Ninoy Aquino International Airport before my departing flight was called to pay a visit on an old friend, Philippine National Police Lieutenant Manny Rodriguez. During my assignment to Manila Station, Manny had been my only recruitment—the most senior PNP officer at NAIA, a man with unfettered access to everything and everyone at the airport.

For two years, for only three hundred dollars a month, Manny, code name Destrier, inserted Immigration Service stamps into Station officers' alias passports. Then, using his PNP auditing software, Manny hacked into the airport's databases and entered false arrival and departure data on the nonexistent travels of these fictitious people. On two occasions, Destrier managed to separate "criteria country" diplomatic couriers, despite their vociferous protests, from their sealed pouches and, with the airport's x-ray equipment, ascertained for Manila Station the top-secret contents of these protected shipments.

Manila Station management enjoyed Manny's services, took all manner of credit for his successes, but then downplayed his import when it came time to prepare my performance evaluations. Margaret, my lumbering branch chief, who had conked me over the head with the bad news about Stan's injuries, felt it necessary to explain the facts of life to me: Destrier was a trifling "support asset," not an esteemed "foreign intelligence producer." As corpulent Maggie imparted this wisdom, I recalled privately that the Station's best FI producer was an expert on Philippine taxation policies. Ho-hum. Just how that agent helped to protect our nation Big Maggie failed to define.

(As an aside, I would like to point out that I found Margaret quite enigmatic because, in my experience, homely women usually have decent personalities.)

Back when I'd told Manny about my transfer to Rome, he'd steadfastly refused to accept turnover to another Station officer, explaining that he had performed these illicit activities only for me, not for the U.S. government. (Though in retrospect, I wonder if I had perhaps insinuated to agent Destrier that he could trust none of my bumbling, self-important colleagues.) Then Manny, shaking my hand goodbye, had offered to facilitate, into perpetuity, my passage and the passage of my kinsmen through NAIA.

And so I always touched base with the good lieutenant when I flew to the Philippines, always bearing the same gift—a bottle of single-malt scotch and an envelope containing five starchy new Benjamins. Having failed to see Manny upon my arrival as I whisked Giuliana to the comfort and shelter of Sparta, I made sure that I passed him the standard largess on my departure. One never knew when Destrier's special services might again come in handy.

# 13

# CHICANERY

10 February 1995.

I returned to Rome rejuvenated, with great plans to conciliate Santo Tommaso and to extirpate a new, but as yet unidentified, target.

Tom called a branch meeting and solicited a volunteer to chase down an exiled Montenegrin aristocrat who was living in Trieste, serving as a middleman between German chemists and the Libyan government. The aristocrat, eager to rebuild his family's depleted coffers, had set up a front company to purchase fine German chemicals, all precursors for weapons of mass destruction. He'd then resold these toxins at twice the market value to embargoed Libya, the terrorist state that detonated a bomb on Pan American flight 103, killing everyone aboard.

"Sounds perfect for me," I said, raising my hand, evoking a grimace from Tom. "I ran a dirty arms dealer cover back in the late eighties during my Islamabad tour."

My timid colleagues were, in unison, examining a flyspeck pattern on the conference-room ceiling. Meanwhile, Tom had taken on an attractive scarlet hue, and a single pulsing vein had risen on his forehead, running hairline to brow.

"See what kind of document package you can wrangle from Headquarters," he said in my general direction, then turned on his heels and marched out.

\* \* \*

11 February 1995.

The Montenegrin, I learned from background reports, had first ventured into the world of international crime by supplying the Hutu-dominated Rwandan regime with surplus Soviet-era weapons from Eastern Europe.

Then I read the hideous aftermath of the aristocrat's dealings: Using the first shipment of weapons, a Hutu commander named "Kintu" and his ragtag crew had ambushed a refugee camp on a warm January night, murdering seven American aid workers and twenty-nine displaced Tutsis in their sleep. In that very instant, the Montenegrin—the facilitator—was downgraded to a secondary target, and Kintu—the perpetrator—was moved to the top of my list.

I shook my head in disgust, calling to mind the United Nations' too-little-too-late policy toward Rwanda. Why, I asked myself, do we so often hide our eyes to such blatant diablerie? Why does distance seem to lessen our concern for the world's wickedness?

\* \* \*

A month and a half later, as I described in this diary's opening pages, the Hutu commander finally paid for his many sins, which were reckoned in full by Odin's cold wire.

* * *

3 April 1995.

My first day in the office after my productive African vacation. I noticed a mysterious change in the Station's ambience. Whispering abounded and would abruptly cease when I entered a room. And I often caught my colleagues looking askance at me.

* * *

1 May 1995.

My worst fears confirmed. I was summoned to the office of the Chief of Station. Tom was already there, sitting in a straight-back chair off to the COS's right, picking at his nibbled fingernails.

"Have a seat, Hank," the COS said, gesturing toward the big couch that faced his desk at an angle.

I plopped down and crossed my legs. I feigned a casual and carefree attitude, though my gastric juices were hatching an escape plan, an esophageal break-out. I gazed out the big windows of the COS's corner office, regarding the Roman skyline.

"What a view," I said. "I'd never get any work done here. Hell, I'd get a good pair of binoculars and scope out the pretty ladies down on Via Veneto each and every day." In fact, I still had excellent optics, the spy-glass that I'd used to conduct surveillance on the UNJ safehouse.

"You never get any work done as it is," Santo Tommaso said.

The COS glared at Tom, made him squirm and resume his quest for lurking hangnails.

Under normal circumstances, I would have answered Tom's gibe with a retaliatory barrage of cutting sarcasm. But because I was thoroughly unnerved, because my instincts were telling me that I was about to sink up to my eyeballs in muck and mire, I remained silent.

"Any idea why you're here?" the COS asked, his tone intently gentle, which discomfited me still more.

"Obviously not for an exceptional performance award."

That prompted a polite smile from the COS. Then he continued: "We just received a back-channel from the Agency's Counter-Espionage Unit alleging you may be involved in some, well, some off-duty chicanery."

"Some what, sir?"

"Wrongdoing, Hank, possible violations of Agency regulation, maybe even U.S. law."

I felt dizzy and had a sudden urge to urinate, and my gastric juices embarked on their spelunking journey toward freedom. But I'd been in sticky situations before, and I knew I could handle this one. I swallowed hard and took a deep breath.

I screwed up my face into my best quizzical expression and said, "Has Tom been taking inventory of the paperclips and pens again?"

Tom winced but kept his head down and his mouth shut, unwilling to test again the COS's patience with one of his typical ersatz ripostes.

"Much more serious than that, I'm afraid," the COS said. "CEU says that you may be"—he coughed into his fist—"implicated in a number of murders."

Painted into a corner, I reached down for my best acting skills and let loose with a roaring belly laugh. My apparent good humor was contagious: The COS soon began to chuckle along with me. Even stoic Santo Tommaso managed a grin and a single snort.

When I'd finally gotten myself back under control, I wiped my tearing eyes and said, "Where's the hidden camera, chief?"

"It's ludicrous, I know," the COS said, "but CEU has latched onto this theory and won't let it go. You're being recalled to Headquarters, immediately, short of tour."

# 14

# MERRIMAC

9 May 1995.

I was assigned to work at Headquarters among a group of quirky, paranoid officers on the North Korea Operations desk. Though the work was highly sensitive and my loyalty was in grave doubt, in retrospect I see that my appointment to NKO was a stroke of genius. The desk was a veritable hermitage, and its officers had a reputation for keeping an eye on one another. And I sensed that, upon my arrival, a good many of those eyes had been instructed to focus on me.

My second day on the job, my Green Line—the internal secure telephone—rang, and a gruff male voice beckoned me to the Counter-Espionage Unit. As I walked, hands clasped behind my back, from the Original Headquarters Building to its bigger and newer counterpart, my nervous mind launched salvo after salvo of morbid thoughts, all portending my personal doomsday.

I hesitated a moment at CEU's doorway and then took a deep breath and marched in. A secretary, the gatekeeper, pointed me toward the appropriate cubicle.

"Have a seat, Mr. Anlaf," the unlikely owner of the whiskey baritone said. He was emaciated, about five-and-a-half-feet tall, with a sweep-over hairstyle and thick spectacles.

He extended his hand over a very cluttered desk and said, "Jim Marinac."

I shook the offered slimy fish and said, "Merrimac, like the Civil War armored boat? How unusual." I was hoping to throw him off balance with some inane banter.

"That's Marinac," he said, a tone of irritation to his voice.

"The nemesis of the Monitor."

"I said 'mare-in-ack.'"

"Exactly. A fantastic sea-battle, so I've read. Your first name is Jim, right?"

The corner of his mouth began to twitch. He said, "Jim, yes, you can call me Jim. Mind if I call you Hank?"

"I'd prefer Mr. Anlaf, really."

The twitching was joined by some robust earlobe pulling. "Are you aware, Mr. *Anlaf*, of the charges against you?"

"Charges!" I sprang from my seat and glared down at Marinac. "I've heard nothing of official charges!"

He was tugging and twitching at an alarming rate. "I-I misspoke," he said. "Allegations, I meant."

I eased myself back into my chair. "What is the source of these absurd accusations, Mr. Merrimac?"

Marinac released his poor crimson earlobe and snatched a photostatic copy from the patchwork carpet of papers on his desk. "A wire service has asserted that the Odin assassinations are the work of a sanctioned or rogue American operative. We're now under some pressure from Congress to investigate the matter."

"Very well, but it remains unclear to me why CEU would want to question an experienced field case officer about a criminal matter."

"Think of CEU as the Agency's internal police." The facial tick disappeared, and Marinac put on a thin smile. "Right now, we're policing you."

"You wouldn't be the first government employee to waste the taxpayers' money."

"Let me tell you what we've found. Then you can decide if we've squandered public funds. You see, Mr. Anlaf, before the news article was published, the Agency received a name-trace request from the Egyptian external service, asking for any available information on a first-name-unknown El-Gamal, citizen of Cyprus, mixed heritage, late thirties. The Egypt desk, however, had no indices matching that description."

My heart was racing, threatening to leap from my chest. But drawing on my facility in the art of misrepresentation, I was able to maintain a placid, indifferent façade.

"The Egyptians later came back to us," Marinac said, "this time with a few more details. They said El-Gamal was wanted in connection with the Odin assassination of the four UNJ terrorists in Aswan. Surely you've heard of those killings?"

I shrugged.

"Around the same time we got the Egyptians' follow-on request, this article"—Marinac waved the paper—"hit the newsstands, and our Legislative Branch went into a collective conniption. The CIA told the Egyptians for a second time that we had nothing on El-Gamal. But CEU was ordered to stand up a task force and investigate the charges."

"Perhaps we should try to avoid using that word, 'charges.'"

"Allegations, then."

I nodded in approval. "So Task Force Odin was born. Old need-to-know TFO. Top secret, hush-hush."

I could see, even through the thick lenses, that his eyes had widened. "Where did you hear that name?"

"I guessed," which was true.

Marinac stared into my eyes, inspecting me for any sign of mendacity. Then he stiffened his posture and slipped on his most reproachful gaze. "I should tell you, *Henry*, CEU has since determined that you were apparently in Cyprus during the UNJ murders. But we haven't yet covertly retrieved the flight manifests for the foreign air carriers servicing Cairo from Nicosia. Once we do, we may very well find some illuminating details regarding your movements during that time frame."

"You're again dancing along that dangerous edge of leveling charges," I said.

"All a matter of interpretation," he said, sounding too self-assured for my taste. "With procurement of the manifests on hold, CEU moved on to analyze the other killings credited to Odin. The assassin's first claimed hit came in January 1993 in Manila. New People's Army commander Manag. Starting to see a pattern here?"

"Indeed," I said, regarding Marinac's wispy comb-over, "male pattern, to be specific." No matter how hard I tried, I continued to engage in such mockery, knowing full well that it might be my downfall. Spouting satire was my habit, just as was gambling and extracurricular homosexuality for the late Fenil Manag.

"You," he said, his voice low and menacing, "were in Manila at the time. So too was one of your friends, a case officer named Bauer, who was critically injured in a terrorist attack on the Embassy."

"*Best* friend, Merrimac. As for my coincidental presence, a lot of other people were there too: the ambassador, the chief of station, even a senior senator on a CoDel"—Congressional Delegation, an overseas junket for a lawmaker and his favored staff.

"But none of them had a motive or the means," Marinac said. "You, on the other hand, had both. A shame the Filipino police buried Manag so quickly; we could've used some ballistic data."

I appreciated Marinac's unintentional divulgence of one of the holes in CEU's case against me.

"Now we move on to Japan," Marinac said. "An old Japanese war criminal gets his throat cut on his living-room floor."

"That Odin sure gets around."

"Apparently so do you. The murder occurred in September 1994, during your scheduled stopover en route from Manila to Rome."

I leaned forward. "Maybe this Odin character is following *me* around. Maybe he's trying to pin the rap on a CIA man, the perfect fall guy." I gasped in shock and realization. "Or maybe the clever bastard is trying to kill *me*. Merrimac, I need protection."

"Or maybe Odin is Elvis, who shows up next in— guess where."

"Graceland?"

"Rome, just like you. Kills a Mafioso in a dark alley, reason unknown."

"Because he was a Mafioso?"

"Perhaps," Marinac said, "but our analysis of Odin suggests that he's a man of principle, that he kills for what he considers to be a bigger purpose."

So just maybe, I was willing to admit to myself, all of these sniveling CEU guys weren't complete morons.

"Which brings us to the UNJ hit, followed more recently by the murder of Sinda Kintu, a former Hutu commander from Rwanda."

Sinda, I thought, how beautiful. I hadn't ever learned that target's real first name, addressed him internally only as Kintu, externally as Monsieur Dubois, his alias in exile. Sinda Kintu sounded to me like a huggable character from an African fairytale. Sometimes the assassination business seemed to me filled with strange little ironies.

"By my math," Marinac said, "that's a total of eight hits."

"Five," I said. "Eight deaths, five hits."

"For an Agency case officer, you seem to know an awful lot about assassination."

"Just a fan of gangster movies. Like, 'Guido, I want you to hit those two guys tonight.' One hit, two guys. Get the idea?"

"Very cute. You seem unaware, Henry, just how much trouble you're in."

My best ideas often come to me in a flash, not after long hours of pondering. Remember how I discovered the water-roller firebomb in Egypt? So it was, as I sat gazing at Marinac's expansive forehead, that I had another marvelous brainstorm.

"Sorry for coming off as flippant, Mr. Marinac," I said, pronouncing his surname carefully. "At first I thought your allegations were too outlandish for me to take seriously." I folded my hands together, put my elbows on the edge of Marinac's desk, and rested my chin on my knuckles. "But this is serious. I suppose I ought to get a lawyer."

Marinac took electricity, just like the boy in the village outside Aswan when I hinted that I was an Egyptian government agent. Marinac said, "I don't think that's necessary just yet, Mr. Anlaf. But of course we, uh, I mean the Office of General Counsel, they can recommend a number of cleared attorneys should you desire...um, any legal advice."

"I prefer not to eat where I shit, Mr. Marinac. Pardon my language. I'll ask our family attorney to recommend a good criminal lawyer, whose name I'll then submit to OGC for full clearances. I have a feeling I'll need to present my chosen advocate with a complete picture of my activities, including classified work. After all, you contend that I corrupted Agency operations for my own purposes. Details of those operations and my involvement in them will be crucial, no doubt, to my counsel's defense. Plus, he'll have to know what he can and cannot tell the media. An investigation into Odin will be very big news."

I sat up straight, smiled, and clapped my hands. "My, this is exciting, isn't it?"

I hadn't seen the blood drain so quickly from someone's face since I stabbed the Neapolitan pimp in the neck.

# 15

# HONEYTRAP

19 May 1995.

I strapped on my Egyptian eye patch and asked Betty Alvarez if she'd ever dated a pirate.

She looked everywhere but at me and said, "A second-story man, yes, but not a pirate."

Her sense of humor was a pleasant surprise to me. She was usually so shy and quiet.

"Swashbucklers are much more exciting than petty thieves, that I promise."

Betty's bony chest heaved, as if she were on the verge of hyperventilating. She managed a quick glance in my direction and said, "What do pirates eat when they go out, grog and hardtack?"

Thus began my courtship of Betty Alvarez—bookish, in her middle thirties, who came and went every day without anyone taking notice. But I did. I originally approached her not for romance but for her access to privileged information. In the end, I got both.

Betty worked in a tiny, windowless office, little more than a closet, deep within the vaulted suite of North Korea Operations. Her supervisor was a hairy-faced old woman who administered NKO's "Special Projects Branch." Inside SPB, Betty's portfolio was called "the ER," which I originally interpreted as involving blown cases, damage control, operational triage, that sort of thing.

But then I overheard a conversation between the overall NKO chief and the bearded lady in which they called Betty's office "Exfiltration and Resettlement." That intriguing title alone inspired me to ask bashful little Betty out for an evening of flowers, good food, witty banter, and a shower of appropriate compliments.

*　　*　　*

10 June 1995.

Our inaugural rendezvous led to several subsequent encounters, which led three weeks later to an illuminating pillow-talk session. On that night, Betty confessed that I was her first lover since college, when she reluctantly surrendered to the persistent and clumsy advances of an aeronautical engineering student. Then, with the reckless abandon that often follows passion (particularly after a long overdue release), she confided to me the sordid details of her most recent exfiltration and resettlement case.

"I saw an adult film last week," Betty said, giggling, snuggling, "for the first time in my life."

"I hear tell that ribald bachelorette parties are *de rigueur* these days. A friend of yours getting married?"

"I didn't see it at a party but at work, believe it or not." Her cheeks colored, and she turned away from me. "Pak Sang-Il, my new orphan, he loves pornography. Can't get enough of it. I had to bring a stack of videos to the safehouse last week. Mr. Pak insisted that I stay and talk, and then he played one of the tapes right in front of me. I was mortified."

"I heard that many North Koreans are secretly obsessed with voluptuous blondes."

"Mr. Pak couldn't care less about Teutonic beauty. He apparently prefers Latinas and Southeast Asians. According to the file, he worked in North Korea's embassies in Mexico and Thailand—and lucky me, I'm half Hispanic. Partway through the film, lover boy puts his hand on my thigh and bats his eyes at me a few times. I got up and left, told him I had pressing business back at Headquarters."

"Did you report him?"

Betty shook her head. "He's just confused. As I was leaving, I could see in his eyes that he was sorry for having offended me. He's a fish out of water, doesn't know what's right and wrong. Like most North Koreans, even the ones who've traveled overseas, he thinks America is the land of anything-goes."

"The Agency doesn't do much resettlement these days," I said, trying to steer the conversation back onto its original trajectory. "Too expensive, I've heard, not enough bang for the buck, a real drain on resources in a time of shrinking budgets."

Probably out of habit, Betty glanced furtively around her cramped studio apartment, as if looking for an eavesdropper. Then she whispered, "Nothing's too expensive for Mr. Pak Sang-Il. When he was in Bangkok, he masterminded the bombing of that South Korean airliner, the one carrying all those American GIs on an excursion trip from Seoul. After that, Mr. Pak went back to Pyongyang and began directing seaborne infiltration missions into South Korea. He's the most senior North Korean Intelligence Service defector we've ever had."

I seethed at the memory of that airliner bombing. Some two dozen of our servicemen had gone down with the plane after it took off from Bangkok on its return flight to Korea. I was again exercising my considerable powers of self-control: This Korean Communist turd had waged covert war against my country and, adding insult to injury, had made a pass at my girl. It was as if he'd devoted his life to pissing me off.

I clenched my fists under the covers and asked casually, "Why would such a man volunteer to work for the Great Imperialist Enemy?"

"He says he finally lost faith in the Dear Leader, says the country is close to economic collapse. Plus, he no longer had to worry about his family being punished for his betrayal. His wife and two children died last year in a train derailment near the Chinese border. But I've looked into that man's gleaming eyes, and I think he just wants a taste of the good life."

Though I was none too comfortable with the idea of working on my native soil, I decided then and there that I would give the murderous Mr. Pak a taste of something else—Odin's garrote.

*    *    *

By prohibiting the use of sex and blackmail in its operations, the CIA has, I think, hobbled itself. In my experience, as the preceding text attests, the "honeytrap" proved to be a most effective—and, in the case of Betty, very enjoyable—targeting and elicitation tool.

With little effort and few resources, I acquired sensitive insights concerning the whereabouts and personality of defector Pak Sang-Il, for which a typical security service would have paid handsomely. But this precious information cost me only six mediocre dinners, two bouquets of roses, and a few nights of mutually satisfying ardor. Then, without my asking, the family jewels had been dropped into my hand—much like what had happened in Rome, when the UNJ report, with its magnificent geo-coordinates, had scrolled unbidden across my computer screen.

I have found that spies often place too great an emphasis on earning their keep through active manipulation and dissembling when they should instead simply lend their ear to a mouth in need of babbling. From Betty's mouth, in addition to secrets, came the thoughts and dreams of a keen, supple mind; she revealed to me the gritty carbon of potential, which—I'll say at the risk of sounding grandiloquent and smug—I encouraged her to press into a radiant diamond of fulfillment. And as Betty blossomed, so too did my fondness for her, though intuition told me that my time with her would be short.

Despite my dark prescience, I stayed close by Betty's side long after tracking down Mr. Pak, for I enjoyed her genuinely and immensely. Also, I confess, her purity, wit, and spare figure reminded me of Giuliana, whose memory served as a stalwart anchor against the tempest that comprised my double life.

# 16

# DOPPELGANGER

12 June 1995.

Marinac's discrepant baritone bid me again to his office. Ten minutes later, I was peering at him over his desk's teetering tribute to disorder.

"So, Henry, did you submit a lawyer's name to the Office of General Counsel?" A lipless smile grew on Marinac's ornithic face, accentuated by the cockscomb of his coifed hair-turban.

I gave him the answer he already knew: "Never got around to it." Actually, I never intended to get around to it. While the CIA's pusillanimity and frigid posturing repulsed me, I internally refused, on principle, to follow through with my threat of exposing some of America's greatest secrets in a court of law.

"Once you *do* get around to retaining counsel, tell him or her that the Department of Justice will pursue any motion or suit filed on your behalf as the initiatory action of an espionage case. DOJ will thereinafter invoke all national security protections afforded by such manner of proceedings." Marinac's metronomic tempo suggested recitation of someone else's words.

"A most masterful display of puppetry, Merrimac. I couldn't even see the strings."

The twitchy canary transformed magically into an irritated weasel—dark eyes narrowed, nostrils flared, elongated incisors bared. Perhaps, I thought, Jim Marinac should have instead devoted his career to field operations, where he could've used his rodent doppelganger to good effect.

"All silly musings about DOJ involvement aside," I said, wearing a mask of insouciance, "why did you really ask me here?"

Marinac patted his crown, taming a disobedient strand, and said, "We're convening a Senior Review Panel to scrutinize your case, analyze all the evidence, and decide if CEU's charges should result in internal administrative action or external litigation."

From my shirt pocket I extracted an index card and my trusty Mont Blanc pen and acted as if I were scribbling a note to myself. "That word, 'charges'—it carries so much weight."

Marinac rolled his eyes, sighed, and pushed back from his desk. "I stand corrected, yet again. Allegations."

I looked up from my card and said, "It's wrong of you to assume that I've failed to solicit legal advice."

My words seemed to goose poor Marinac, for he jerked up straight in his chair. Then he cocked an ear toward me, the lobe of which he began to tug at an alarming rate.

"I talked to one of my buddies who used to work for OGC," I continued, "and he or she said the Agency's legally beholden to grant me discovery of the details of the case being built against me."

The "buddy" was actually sweet and concerned Betty, and her association with the Office of General Counsel consisted of a one-month training interim back when she first joined the Agency. She wasn't completely certain of her legal opinion but considered it plausible enough to form the basis of a bluff.

Marinac avoided eye contact and began to fiddle with the clutter of papers on his desk. I took his disengagement and fidgeting as likely confirmation that either Betty had been correct or Marinac, not knowing any better, had fallen for her sketchy contrivance.

"I hope you're looking for the case summary," I said.

Still not looking at me, Marinac snatched a folder from his computer table and held it toward me. I took the file and flipped it open: a single page, a poor quality photostatic copy of a document with four vertical columns of romanized surnames. A number-letter pair—such as "10A"—was typed next to each name, as was a small handwritten checkmark. Someone, probably a flight attendant, had scrawled several lines of undecipherable Arabic script in the document's margins. My eyes were drawn to seat 7G (my lucky number, seven, which was an aisle seat, as I recall), occupied by one "Elgamal." The name was high-lighted—by Marinac, I assumed—with bright yellow ink.

I handed the folder back to Marinac. "So this is all you've got, a piece of paper with a name that happens to be the same as one of my operational aliases?"

"We've also got a covert affidavit testifying to the document's date and chain of custody. DOJ says it's admissible." The canary was back, still twitchy, but smiling more broadly than I'd ever seen before. "But unless you begin to act on your threat to hire an attorney, we couldn't care less about this piece of paper, Henry. We've already got sufficient circumstantial evidence to downgrade your clearances and stick you someplace where you can't do any more harm to the organization."

I sprang from the chair. "I've never harmed this Agency or my country, you little prick."

Marinac looked terrified. After all, he was convinced that I was Odin, the ruthless international assassin. Come to think of it, since his conclusions about me were dead-on accurate, he had every right to be scared. But I wasn't in this game to inflict injury on my fellow patriots, no matter how misinformed, petty, and cowardly they might be.

I dropped back into my seat and waited for Marinac to reassemble what passed for his dignity. When he did, he had another surprise for me: "The Senior Review Panel has no legal charter or jurisdiction; they only consider suitability issues. And you have a long and colored past on that subject."

So *that* was it, I thought. The bastards weren't building a legal case against me. The standard for that was much too high. They were going to muckrake, to bare my checkered past. My womanizing (on Sparta), my unsanctioned time away from work (studying jujitsu, fleeing Santo Tomasso to the streets of Rome), my professional failures (not following through with Hassan in Cyprus, the Montenegrin in Trieste)—the Panel would use all of these damning facts to drum me out of the service.

"You are to report to work at the Intelligence Library immediately," Marinac said. "Your personal effects from NKO are being transferred there now."

I rose and shuffled over to the cubicle's opening, as if I were sadly conceding victory to the bird-vermin hybrid. Then I stopped abruptly at the threshold, turned around, and said, "You and your cat, Merrimac, how do the two of you like living in that townhouse off Route Seven in Falls Church?" Since he already believed I was Odin, I thought I'd derive at least some small satisfaction from his fears.

I wasn't disappointed: Marinac stared at me, mouth agape, refracted eyes wide with alarm. "W-what did you just say?" he whispered.

Without another word, I swiveled back around and strode through the walkway, past the glaring gate-keeper, and out into the main corridor.

\* \* \*

How, you might ask, did I know those details of Marinac's pitiful life? Simple deduction. During our first encounter, I noticed white animal hair on his clothing, and I later found his name and address in the telephone book. I went with the stereotype that a weak little man like Marinac would own a cat or small dog, a pet that wouldn't intimidate him and over which even he could establish dominance. And, at the last moment, going on a hunch, I guessed cat.

\* \* \*

With my exile to the Intelligence Library and with the end of my career so clearly in sight, I was com-mitted to one final act in my consecrated mission. I would leave the Agency in a blaze of glory, taking with me Pak Sang-Il, the former NKIS mastermind, who now spent his days watching porn and groping his female CIA handlers.

But before I had the chance to schedule Pak's appointment with the Grim Reaper, I received the most devastating news of my life.

# 17

# PORNOGRAPHY

16 June 1995.

On weekday mornings, Betty Alvarez often drove from her condominium apartment to one of three safehouses that held the North Korean defectors for which she was responsible. Because I had volunteered for the Intelligence Library shift that ran from noon to eight o'clock *post meridiem*, I was available to conduct surveillance on Betty almost every day.

Working alone, without the support of a trained surveillance team, I frequently lost Betty in the heavy brambles of traffic within and around the Washington Beltway. But I was persistent and, over the course of two weeks, tracked her to each of the three safehouses, though I remained unsure which one Mr. Pak occupied. I was, however, very certain of one fact: All of the houses had extensive security. At each I spotted closed circuit cameras and electrified fences and motion detectors, and Betty was admitted only after being scrutinized by a safehouse keeper, who, I assumed, was an Agency security officer.

★ ★ ★

28 July 1995.

On my seventh, lucky week of trailing Betty, I watched her depart from the safehouse that was nestled behind a stone wall and stands of tall trees in the upscale Great Falls area of northern Virginia. I followed her car to a strip mall in Tysons Corner. Carrying a small shopping bag, Betty walked into a boutique called "Titillarama" and exited five minutes later, the bag folded and stuffed in her purse.

I waited for her to pull out of the parking lot and then wandered over to the store. Upon entering, I was greeted by a shocking floor-to-ceiling display of skin-tone sex toys, bawdily titled films, and shapeless doily-cloth negligees. After I reeled my eyeballs back into their sockets, I fell into character and ambled over to the counter, behind which stood a middle-aged, platinum-blonde woman with green cobweb-pattern tattoos on her forearms.

"Need some help?" she asked with a raspy smoker's voice.

"My girlfriend—slender, dark features—just now dropped off some videos."

"She's a regular."

"But painfully shy. She admitted to me only last week that she enjoys adult films, started watching them back when she was single. But she's still too embarrassed to tell me exactly which genres she likes."

"The *what* she likes?"

My near-perfect French pronunciation of "genres" had thrown the spider-lady for a loop. "Types, kinds. You know, like girl-on-girl, interracial."

The spider-lady nodded, reached down under the counter, and retrieved a stack of four tapes, the cardboard sleeves of which bore startlingly graphic video captures. "This is what she rented day before yesterday."

I sorted through the films—all heterosexual, two starring Latina actresses, two with Thais. I pulled one of the videotapes from its box and discovered two distasteful facts: 1) It hadn't been rewound and 2) It was covered with suspiciously cakey fingerprints and smudges. Mr. Pak, I surmised, terrorist mastermind and aspiring fondler, had, by all indications, thoroughly enjoyed last night's feature presentation.

"One of our most popular south-of-the-border selections," the spider-lady said. "You like it?"

"If this won't float your boat, nothing will. How much?"

"Five to rent for two nights, twenty-five to purchase." She regarded the grubby remnants of Mr. Pak's handling and added, "I can get you a shrink-wrapped copy from out back."

"Sold to the man beside the French Ticklers!"

\*   \*   \*

I swung by my apartment to drop off the videotape and to slip into some fresh clothes before heading off to my thrilling job of tidying the stacks at the Intelligence Library. As was my usual practice, I inspected the entire flat for any telltale signs of surreptitious entry by the CIA or FBI (a standard practice in "espionage" cases) but found none.

On my way out the door, I happened to glance at my answering machine. The message light was flashing at a furious rate. This came as quite a surprise,

since Betty usually contacted me at work, and my
father called only on weekends—unless a serious
problem had arisen. My arms erupted in goosebumps.
I tapped the retrieval button and waited breathlessly as
the mini-cassette rewound.

Irene's voice, panicky: "Hank, please call me as
soon as you can. Stan's having trouble breathing. I
contacted Makati Medical, and they're sending a military helicopter. Call me when you get this."

Four similar messages from Irene followed but
offered me no further details. Then came the sixth.
Whereas seven was my lucky number, six had always
been a thorn in my side, a bloody gauntlet through
which I had to pass to reach my good fortune.

"Hank, this is Imelda"—my favorite green-armband girl, Irene's fellow Elder and best friend on
Sparta—"The helicopter just left, took Stan and Irene
to Makati. H-he stopped breathing a few minutes
before it arrived. The medics, they revived him, put
him on a respirator. Stan is.... You should come right
away, Hank. We all love you."

The machine beeped three times, signaling the
end of recorded messages, and reset itself. Stunned by
this unexpected turn of events, I stared at the pulsing
red beacon, which had been the unlikely augury of my
worst nightmares. I eventually shook off my bewilderment and called my supervisor at the Intelligence
Library. I told the tennis-shoe-clad old lady that my
best friend was seriously ill and that I wanted to catch
the next plane to the Philippines to be with him.

"I'm so sorry, Hank," she said. "Yes, of course, you
must go immediately. I'll take care of the paperwork."

As I hung up the receiver, I found small comfort
in one fact: Stan's loving parents would be spared this
dreadful news. His father had recently passed from a

massive heart attack, and shortly thereafter, Stan's mother, unable to cope with the loss of her husband, had slipped into the viscid brume of dementia. No longer aware of the world around her, she now resided in an asylum on the outskirts of Sacramento.

In some cases, I thought, mental illness served as a shield, protecting a friable mind from life's most vicious blows.

# 18

# VALHALLA

29 July 1995.

During my long flight to the other side of the
world, I composed a few lines of hackneyed verse for
Giuliana in her native tongue:

*Il Domatore Del Timone*

*Lo spirito dell'antenato domatore del timone*
  *vive ancora all'interno di me*
*I miei occhi si fissano sulle risacche distanti*
*Il ponte dondola sotto i miei piedi*
*Il cielo passa al disopra della mia testa*
*La mia posizione in questa estensione e certa*
*Ma il mio destino e sconosciuto*

*Il timone tira per essere libero dalla mia stretta*
*La corrente si oppone e mi forza ad*
  *abbandonare la mia resistenza*
*C'e una ninta con I cappelli neri che guida*
  *la mia anima*
*Le sue sottili e tetre dita serrano il mio cuore*
*Il vento fragrante e fresco riempie la mia vela*
*Non importa dove vengo trasportato*

*Ho imparato gli umori del mare*
*Lei insegnava le cose che la mia vita ha*
  *trascurato*
*L'ammaliatrice eterea mi ha compiuto*
*Lei ha approfondito la mia anima placida*


Having proved that even schoolboy drivel sounds
wonderful in Italian, I translated the poem into
English on the reverse side of the paper:

*The Helmsman*

*The spirit of a long-dead helmsman lives within*
  *me*
*My eyes affix on the distant swell line*
*The deck it pitches beneath*
*The sky it passes above*
*My place in this expanse is certain*
*But my destiny is unknown*

*The rudder strains to be free of my grasp*
*The sea-stream makes me abandon resistance*
*It is the raven-haired siren who guides my soul*
*Her slender, dark fingers hold my heart*
*Sweet, cool wind fills my sail*
*It matters not where I am taken*

*I have learned the ways of the sea*
*She has taught me what life neglected*
*The rare beauty has fulfilled me*
*She has deepened my placid soul*

\*   \*   \*

Reading again my doggerel, I feel my face grow warm from embarrassment. But I realize now, with the insight that comes only with the passage of time, that my composition was spawned not by my unrequited love for Giuliana but by my sorrow about Stan, my best friend, who was at that very moment struggling for his life. So unable was I to tell Stan how much I valued his unwavering friendship that I took up my pen and instead declared my devotion to an acceptable proxy: my gypsy princess.

\*   \*   \*

2 August 1995.

Stan died two days after I arrived in Manila. He never opened his eyes, but during my first hour by his side, he once squeezed my hand, acknowledging my presence.

When the attending physician announced Stan's passing, I felt as if my insides suddenly liquefied and spilled out, leaving behind a shattered, useless vessel. With my body no longer able to provide secure anchorage, my soul, my very essence, drifted away.

I peered down from the ceiling at my worldly self, which stood beside Stan's hospital bed, teetering back and forth, threatening to collapse. My body's eyes, glassy and set in an ashen face, flicked upward and stared at me. The listless gaze enveloped me, gripped me, and then, much to my surprise, winched me back down. Once again mated with my maladroit body, I began gulping for air, overcome with the fear that at any moment I might slip beneath the whitecaps of despair and sink into the depths of madness—or, as some would contend, *greater* madness.

I was not alone in my desperation. The trauma threw heartbroken Irene into an excruciating labor. Ten hours later, she delivered a healthy baby boy, who, by previous agreement with Stan, she named Henry. This unanticipated sprouting of life from the barren plains of death shook both Irene and me from our suffocating grief.

A doe-eyed nurse handed the swaddled newborn to me and said, "He has your nose."

I kissed Henry on his forehead and laid him in the crook of his exhausted mother's arm. "Not likely," I said, smiling at Irene, "since I only arrived from America a couple of days ago. But I am his godfather."

After the nurse and doctor departed, Irene said, "Stan's health improved for a few months after you left. He was so happy when I became pregnant."

I realized that Irene was asking for my help to make real her myth about Henry's parentage. I touched the baby's tiny, curled hand.

"Knowing that he had given you a piece of himself," I said, "perhaps Stan felt that he could finally surrender to God's persistent calls."

With tears in her eyes, Irene placed her hand, warm and dry as always, even after hours of labor, on top of mine and said, "Stan understood how much you wanted him to be happy and"—she glanced at Henry—"he cherished what you did for him."

Having thus absolved me of any possible guilt, from that day forward Irene only spoke of Henry as Stan's miracle child.

\*    \*    \*

9 August 1995.

While waiting for Stan's embalmed remains to be flown and ferried to Sparta, I commissioned the construction of a scaled-down Viking dragon boat, a clinker-built craft with carved serpents adorning its towering prows fore and aft.

Working from my copies of Oslo Museum photographs, the skilful shipwrights of the Cuyo Islands Fishermen's Federation assembled the fifteen-foot "longship" in only one week, though they would have required another fortnight to make the vessel watertight and to fashion a mast and workable square sail. But for the boat's maiden and final voyage, I told the craftsmen, it need not be seaworthy.

I also hired a local machete-maker to fabricate a Viking longsword and wooden scabbard, into which I carved a runic approximation of Stan's name. While the local workers fulfilled my contracts, I drove myself to exhaustion by digging a long and deep hole on the crest of Mount Athena, where Stan's son Henry had been conceived.

During that entire week of waiting and laboring, I never once saw Giuliana. The other girls told me she was recovering from a brief but unspecified illness, had quarantined herself, but would definitely attend Stan's funeral. Something about that explanation didn't ring true, but I was too busy and distraught to contemplate the matter further.

★   ★   ★

10 August 1995.

Lifting out the last shovel of dirt, I heard the growling diesel engines of the ferry that I had chartered in Puerta Princessa, the capital city of nearby Palawan Island, to bring Stan's body to Sparta. By the time I descended Mount Athena, the ferryboat's attendants had off-loaded the casket, which was now surrounded by all of Sparta's citizens, save Giuliana. Everyone was weeping. I paid the ferry crew the remainder of the agreed fee and added a generous tip for their respectful handling of my friend's remains.

I jogged down to the beach and asked the shipwrights to haul the longship to the island's highest point and to position it in the large hole dug there. Then I returned to the grieving crowd and selected five of the younger girls to help me carry the coffin to the summit of Athena.

As we trudged up the narrow trail, Irene, cradling Henry, fell in behind us, followed by a single-file string of mourners. At the halfway point, I glanced back and saw Giuliana, her complexion sallow and her figure even bonier than usual, lagging several paces back from the end of the line. I also noticed that all of the girls were holding leis of fragrant sampaguita, a variety of jasmine that is the national flower of the Philippines. It was as if the leis had appeared from nowhere, though I guessed that someone had slipped away en route to retrieve the garlands.

When we reached the summit, the longship was lying in my deep trench, and beside it, on a strip of white cloth, the blacksmith had placed the longsword. We gently set the casket down on the boat's plank floor, and then I laid the sword lengthwise on the coffin lid.

I walked to the crest of Mount Athena and stood at ship's bow. Fixing my eyes on the head of my friend's simple pine box, I quoted a stanza from the ninth-century poem *Havamal*, the words of which were attributed to the Norse god Odin:

*Possessions die,*
*Kindred die,*
*A man himself*
*Must also die;*
*But glory*
*Will never die*
*For a man who*
*Achieves it well.*

"Valhalla is much greater," I concluded, "for your having left us, dear friend."

(I should note that Valhalla was, to me, simply a generic reference to Heaven, not to some specific pagan afterworld. Also, to my knowledge, Stan Bauer had no claim to Scandinavian ancestry, but still, if ever a man deserved a Viking-warrior funeral, he did.)

Then I moved over to the tall pile of excavated earth, picked up my shovel, and started backfilling the trench. With Irene and Henry watching, the girls—including Giuliana—gathered around me and, using their hands, began scooping dirt over the longship. Two hours later, what had taken me days to dig out was refilled.

Without a word of direction, we formed a circle around Stan's grave, and the girls tossed their sampaguitas onto the Viking burial mound. Imelda handed the largest lei to me, and I placed it on a spot roughly over Stan's head.

One by one, the girls crossed themselves and drifted away down the path to our compound. Irene, Henry, and I were soon left alone on Mount Athena. Henry began to cry, and Irene gave him one of her perfect breasts. That was a boy, I thought, who would grow up to have only the highest standards.

"Will you stay on the island?" I asked.

"Of course," Irene said, directing an affectionate gaze at Henry as he suckled. "This is where Stan and I planned to raise Henry, so this is where our son will be raised."

"Getting a big sister to baby-sit shouldn't be a problem."

Irene looked up at me, and I quickly pried my eyes away from her exposed breast and focused on her face. She said, "Since Stan's death, some of the girls have been talking about leaving. There are many single fishermen on the other islands. The men here are very industrious; they'd make good husbands."

I let that revelation rattle around inside my tormented cranium for a moment before I responded: "It's time the girls settled down to normal lives."

Irene stared at me so hard that I finally had to turn away. She let out a heavy sigh. "I said only *some* of the girls want to leave."

I plucked my Mont Blanc pen from my shirt pocket and began using its nib to scrape dirt from under one of my thumbnails. "So who wants to stay?"

Irene rolled her eyes and, trying hard to indulge me, said, "Two girls. Giuliana is one of them, of course, but she has a serious problem to work through."

That caught my attention. I abandoned my grooming and looked up at Irene. "What's going on?"

"I assume you know she was abused before she came here."

I nodded.

"She's been sickly since you left. A few months ago, she developed jaundice and became too weak to get out of bed. It was time for Stan's next appointment in Manila, so we convinced her to come with us. Stan's doctor confirmed what I already suspected—Giuliana has serum hepatitis."

I wasn't surprised that the filthy pimp had infected her with something. "How is she?"

"Much better now that she's on medication. But it's a chronic disease, Hank, and she'll most likely have complications down the road. If her liver suffers too much damage, she'll need a transplant. Only time will tell."

"I can take her back to specialists in the States," I said as panic began to fill my heart. With Stan's passing so fresh in my mind, I was horrified at the prospect of also losing Giuliana.

"She wants to stay *here*," Irene said sharply, with complete finality, dissuading any argument from me.

"Maybe I'll hang around for a while longer, just to make sure she's on the road to recovery."

"That's exactly what she thought you'd say. Giuliana wants you to return to Washington before you do something foolish like declare your undying devotion to her. She loves you, Hank, and is so grateful for your saving her, but after everything she's been through, she's not looking for romance or a husband and probably never will. She asks only for your care and compassion."

A sense of relief swept over me. Much to my surprise, I found Giuliana's terms for our relationship to be not only acceptable but also preferable. Though she had never solicited my succor, I'd taken on the responsibility for ensuring her happiness. With simple words, Giuliana had plucked from my neck this millstone of my own making.

In place of puerile romanticism, I decided, I would give Giuliana a pure and platonic affection, asking for nothing in return. From me she would learn that not all men were intent on dragging her into a carnal thralldom.

"Like most adolescents," Irene said, interrupting my musing, "you gaze at the pretty wildflowers in the distance while failing to notice the bouquet right under your nose."

"Wha...?" I asked intelligently.

"I said two women, you idiot. The other is Imelda, the woman completely but silently committed to you. You're the first and only man she's ever been with. Holy Mother of God, does a man have to be hobbled before his other senses are wakened?"

"Uh, Imelda...?" I was proving myself to be quite the orator.

Henry was finished with his snack, so Irene tucked that magnificent gland into her blouse. She glared at me and said, "I give up," wheeled around and stomped down the trail toward the main house.

"Uh, Imelda...?"

Irene called back over her shoulder, "Once you finish whatever ugly business you have to do in Washington, think about coming back here and gaining some perspective. Your godson would love to have a little cousin named Stanley or Irene to play with."

"Imelda?" I whispered in bewilderment, thinking of the beautiful toffee-skinned woman who, because of her acumen and fairness and seniority, served with Irene on Sparta's Council of Elders. Imelda and I had shared so many wonderful times together; we were very compatible, in every sense of the word. Why hadn't I recognized the significance of this perfect harmony? I already had the answer: I was an idiot, just as Irene had said.

I had taken Imelda for granted for so long. Was it too late, I asked myself, to make amends for past blunders and insults? I decided quickly that I would talk to her before I left, begging her to forgive me for my neglect, my callousness. If she would have me, even if she would just promise to think about having me, I would pledge to her that I would return as soon as I tied up some loose ends back stateside. Then I would give her an English copy of my poem, for it was she who truly deserved it.

In my mind, I quickly compiled a prioritized list of those loose ends: 1) Confront the Senior Review Panel and, one way or another, force their hand; 2) Gently, very gently, end my relationship with dear sweet Betty; and 3) Choke the craven life out of Pak Sang-Il, murderer and opportunist.

Seeing that I had some pretty heavy action items on my agenda, I decided to get cracking. So, after talking to Imelda and Giuliana, I returned to Washington the very nex day.

# 19

# ENFILADE

14 August 1995.

At one minute past noon on the day I returned to work, I received a written summons, complete with a red date/time stamp, to appear at once before an already-convened Senior Review Panel.

I noticed that the provided room number was on the vaunted Seventh Floor of the Original Headquarters Building. This was where the Director of Central Intelligence and his bootlickers maintained their plush offices, while the Agency's worker bees were banished to stifling cubicles, devoid of fresh air, natural light, and even a modicum of elbowroom. In other words, I, a mere serf from the modular dungeons, was being asked to appear before the splendor of the King's Court for judgment and sentencing.

The door to the assigned chamber was open, so in I strode without a moment's hesitation. I wanted my audience to know that I was confident and unafraid of their petty bureaucratic processes.

The room was very large and rectangular, with a massive hardwood table in its center. Seated along one length of this impressive piece of furniture, facing the door, were six elderly gentlemen—all bearing identical stoic expressions. This was an old boys' club, I concluded; no women allowed. At the table's far end was the comparatively cherubic face and familiar comb-over of Jim Marinac. These men were perfectly positioned, I observed, to let loose with an interrogational enfilade.

"Have a seat, Mr. Anlaf," one of the wrinkled codgers said, nodding toward the lone chair on the opposite side of the table.

I raised an eyebrow, put on a crooked smile, and complied. I heard the door click shut and turned but saw no one; perhaps a minion had come silently from the hall.

The same man—perhaps the most senior of the seniors—said, "I now declare this Senior Review Panel in session." He and the other men paused to scribble on the papers before them.

"This panel has been convened," the man continued, "to discuss the case of Mr. Henry Ivar Anlaf, employee number two-four-one-three-six-five, a field operations officer home-based with the Near East Division of the Directorate of Operations." More synchronized scribbling.

"Mr. Anlaf appears before us," he said, "to answer a number of corroborated reports that he has engaged repeatedly in activities unbecoming an officer of this Agency. Based on the nature of these accusations, the panel seriously questions Mr. Anlaf's suitability for continued employment with this organization. Do you have any questions or comments, Mr. Anlaf, before we proceed?"

I realized that this was a show trial, convened to announce a verdict that had been reached days, weeks, perhaps months before in the Seventh Floor's inner sanctum. I shook my head; I had nothing to say. What could I say?

A graybeard—he actually had a gray beard—on the far right spoke next. "First we will consider reports of your involvement in overtly salacious behaviors. Please describe your activities on an island in"—the graybeard consulted his notes—"the Cuyo Group in the Philippines."

"My best friend, Stanley Bauer, a former operations officer, was the innocent victim of a terrorist attack in Manila. He suffered horrible injuries that left him paralyzed from the waist down. I established a modest home for him on Pawikan, a previously uninhabited island in the Cuyos, and I hoped that this sanctuary from a dangerous world, this refuge with sultry breezes, swaying palms and solitude, would aid in the recovery of his broken body and spirit. I also wanted him close to me, so we could spend as much time together as possible."

(My custom, rarely noticed by CIA toadies, was to answer banality with euphuism.)

"Solitude?" the graybeard said, incredulous. "What about the dozen young Filipino women you imported to the island?"

"Ten, actually," I said. "And one of them was a registered nurse. The other nine were well-meaning women who volunteered to assist the nurse and attend to the day-to-day household and maintenance chores that Mr. Bauer could no longer perform. I pooled a full third of my life's savings with Mr. Bauer's medical settlement to ensure that he was comfortable and that he received comprehensive and personal care."

"It is an established fact," the graybeard said, "that Mr. Bauer was a paraplegic and was probably unable to indulge in, uh, the attentions of those women. But as for you, we have reports that this 'comprehensive and personal care' was also administered to you. Is it not true that you took advantage of these young and isolated women and convinced a number of them to engage with you regularly in licentious acts?"

"You must understand," I began in a pedagogic tone, as if I were correcting the man's unlearned inference, "I had, quite unintentionally, given purpose and stability to the lives of Mr. Bauer's attendants. They were grateful to me, and I was grateful to them for helping Mr. Bauer. From this came mutual respect. From respect came, predictably, attraction. So, over the course of two years, I—a young, healthy, and single man—was lucky enough to have romantic relationships with some of the girls."

"How many is 'some?'""

"Three," I lied. I had shared intimacies with all five of the girls who'd worn my green armbands, to say nothing of my clandestine union with Irene. "Probably no more," I added, "than many of my colleagues in this very building have enjoyed over that same stretch of time."

"Did you have sexual intercourse with any of these women on your last trip, when you visited the island for Mr. Bauer's funeral?"

"No," I said, telling the truth.

"I see here," one of the other old men said while gazing at a document, "that you failed to follow proper procedure before you last traveled to the Philippines. You left the country without official permission, Mr. Anlaf. That is a serious oversight"—he peered over at the smirking Merrimac—"with very real counter-intelligence implications."

"Following standard operating procedures for personal emergencies, I telephoned my supervisor immediately upon hearing the news of Mr. Bauer's deteriorating condition. I asked for and received her permission to take leave from work and to fly to the Philippines."

The man dug out another document from his sheaf of papers. "According to this sworn and signed affidavit from our head librarian, Mrs. Mary Walker, you did call her, but you ignored her request that you fill out and file a leave slip and that you contact the Office of Security to obtain clearance for your intended overseas travel."

The panel had sunk to a new low—from presenting their warped prejudices as fact to coercing the fabrication of evidence against me. But what should I have expected, fairness? After all, Mrs. Walker had to consider her working conditions and her pension. I opted not to acknowledge or contest this instance of dirty legerdemain and sat quietly, awaiting the next barrage of injustice.

"Do you engage in any acts that may be considered perverse, Mr. Anlaf?" It was the man who had convened the kangaroo court.

"Nothing so described under law. Other than following orders without question and performing acts of espionage for my country. Otherwise, my predilections are quite normal, I think."

The man held up the videotape that I'd purchased in Tysons Corner while following Betty. The bastards had tossed my apartment while I was in the Philippines and, without a hint of shame, were flaunting their plunder before me.

He said, "Some people would consider the viewing of such smut to be aberrant behavior."

"Some people would consider breaking and entering to be aberrant behavior," I said, no longer able to conceal my contempt. "And please don't tell me that none of you has ever voluntarily seen an adult film, or two, or a hundred."

I was confronted with a row of pates, which alternated between bald and hoary, as my panel in unison stared down at their notes, unwilling to meet my eyes.

The lead interrogator was the first to raise his head. He glanced at the videotape's cover and said, "What's the meaning of this title, 'Taco Pies?'"

With my scorn exposed, I had nothing to lose. In a condescending tone, I said, "Simple deduction would suggest it's a crass reference to Hispanic women's genitalia."

"Now we move on," the graybeard interjected, appearing very anxious to change the subject, "to several reports alleging your dereliction of assigned duties."

I looked at each of my interrogators in turn, except for Jim Marinac, but said nothing. From now on, I decided, if they wanted me to provide an answer, they'd have to submit an unambiguous request.

"After getting off to a good start in Manila," the graybeard continued, "you seemed to have dropped the ball, spent most of your time on that island or in some exercise class." He folded his hands and tilted his head to the side. "To be a successful ops officer, one must work countless hours on the street, in mosques, on the different social and diplomatic circuits. You apparently did this at your first two posts but seem to have thrown in the towel when you reached the Philippines. What happened?"

"I pulled two hardship tours before Manila," I began. "Both places were little more than open toilets; living conditions were abysmal. But I not only survived during these assignments—I thrived. I handled both stations' most sensitive sources, I recruited well-placed agents, and I exercised rock-solid tradecraft. I was the go-to man, a reliable old workhorse that never once grumbled or whimpered.

"Shortly before my transfer to the Philippines, I got passed over for promotion for the second time in a row. But two of my colleagues—whose expertise was limited to knowing exactly when to kowtow like a helot★ and when to strut like a peacock—were promoted. So I came to the belated realization that, since I wasn't going to be rewarded for doing my job and doing it well, I might as well focus on other things, like my best friend and my 'exercise classes,' as you called them. Either way I was getting ignored by the Agency, so why break my neck?"

"Not a very corporate view of your place in this organization, Mr. Anlaf. Everyone on this panel has suffered professional setbacks, but none of us has chosen to retire in place." His was a cute play on the Agency jargon "recruitment in place," meaning a spy who'd been convinced to stay in his overt job, maintaining his access, so that he could continue to pilfer secrets for Uncle Sam.

"You're right that I'm not very 'corporate,' *sir*," I answered, a jagged edge to my voice. "That's because I don't work for a fucking corporation. I'm a goddamn field operative for the CIA, not a mealy-mouthed merchant whose one-track mind and myopic eyes are obsessed with some fucking bottom line. As for any of your supposed 'setbacks,' I don't believe for one goddamn second that anyone who's a super-grade in this Agency has ever encountered anything more than a pimple-size bump on their autobahn drive to seniority."

---

★ A slave of ancient Sparta.

My sudden display of anger and purposeful cursing had caught the panel by surprise. Each man's eyes
were wide, and each jaw had dropped. Marinac was in
real danger of suffering a detached earlobe. All of the
men seemed unnerved. No, not unnerved—they
were scared silly. Then it dawned on me: The last
thing that these creaky old farts wanted was to test
their strong suspicions about my lethal disregard of
Executive Order 12333.★ They obviously yearned to
finish this session as quickly and cleanly as possible,
without arousing my alleged homicidal tendencies.

The graybeard proved to be the panel's bravest by
reading again from the registry of my rumored foibles:
"Regardless of your personal feelings about the CIA's
evaluation system"—I noticed a waver in his voice—
"the fact remains that you fell far short of the established objectives for your grade in both the Philippines and Italy. For example, in Rome, you rarely
showed up to work on time; you wandered around
the city for hours; you were consistently tardy in sub-
mitting your operational and intelligence write-ups;
and you took more than your share of vacation time."

He had neglected to ask a question, so I failed to
provide an answer. Instead I glared at him, arms
crossed over my chest, until he sheepishly turned back
to his papers.

"Your personnel file indicates that you're multi-
lingual. Is that correct?" The inquiry had come from
one of the men who hadn't previously spoken.

I suspected that this was a lame attempt to establish rapport with me, to loosen me up a bit, but I saw

---

★ E.O. 12333, Part 2.11: "Prohibition on Assassination.
No person employed by or acting on behalf of the United
States Government shall engage in, or conspire to engage
in, assassination."

no harm in playing along, at least for a while. "I'm not a true polyglot, but I do have a slight facility for learning other tongues."

"Do you have much formal training in foreign languages?"

"My small hometown offered no such courses, but my father encouraged my self-directed study and bought me a number of books and audio tapes."

The old man shuffled through his papers, stopping at one and reading it. "You grew up in Lancaster, Minnesota, near the Canadian border. Mostly Germans there, right?"

"The town's population is largely Scandinavian-American, with a sprinkling of descendants of German and Polish immigrants."

"You mentioned your father. What about your mother?"

"She died from a massive stroke when I was in middle school." This conversation was moving in a very personal direction with which I was uncomfortable, so I took measures to alter its course. "I'm sure that you and your insightful colleagues have concluded that my lifelong, impossible search for my mother's replacement explains my unchecked womanizing and misogyny."

"What a waste," my current inquisitor said, obviously put off by my noxious comment. "Smart, linguistically gifted, from a supportive family. A shame you never rose to your potential, chose to throw it all away." He shook his head, as if he were disappointed with being forced to end what could have been a promising career.

"We'll adjourn now for deliberation," the apparent leader said. "Please return to the library, Mr. Anlaf, and await our decision."

\*     \*     \*

One hour later, after filling out and signing all of the requisite paperwork, I was escorted from the CIA Headquarters building by two stocky Special Police Officers, members of the Agency's guard detail. Mrs. Walker, the head librarian, and Betty were nowhere to be found as I completed this curt and sterile ritual that signaled the terminus of my nine-year journey with the CIA.

\*     \*     \*

17 August 1995.

In the end, I was spared from having to end my relationship with Betty. My calls to her went unanswered, but I managed to catch her on this morning as she walked from her condominium to her car.

In a trembling voice, she said, "I'll lose my job if we're seen together." Then she jumped into her sedan and sped off.

# 20

# MASSEUSE

27 August 1995.

My sixth masseuse, a portly Thai matron, showed up at my hotel room and immediately pulled down her skin-tight knit shirt, revealing the bulging top half of her bust. On her left breast was a bad tattoo that read "AJ," on the other, "BJ." I could tell at a glance that she was as inappropriate for my plan as were the five women who had preceded her.

"AJ is who I am," she explained without my asking. "Angel Jasmine. BJ is what I do." Then she smiled, revealing a shiny gold incisor.

I took a deep breath and steeled myself. I was determined to give even the most unlikely candidate a fair audition. "All I want is a massage," I said, "nothing else."

Her brow furrowed as she grappled with what I had said. "Just a massage?" she asked in disbelief. "No happy ending?"

Once we'd settled on the truncated terms of her service and on a handsome price, Ms. Jasmine proved that she had no idea whatsoever how to give a rubdown. My shoulders ached for three days after her inept pummeling.

★   ★   ★

30 August 1995.

As always, lucky number seven came through for me. With her nimble fingers dancing across my back, the next and final young lady related her hard-luck biography.

She was a stunning nineteen-year-old native of the northern mountains of Laos. She'd been sold to a Thai brothel in Chiang Mai at the tender age of sixteen. Two years later, an American tourist found her there, liberated her with a proposal of marriage and a large bribe to her masters, and then took her back to Maryland on a fiancée visa.

Her American husband turned out to be a wife-beater. Concerned neighbors reported the abuse, and the man was arrested, tried, and convicted. Because he came to trial with an existing record of domestic violence, the judge sentenced the masseuse's husband to three years in prison.

The masseuse was grateful to the American judicial system for saving her from injury or worse, but she was left with an eviction notice and no income. So she returned to the only profession that she knew.

I contracted for the masseuse's services three more times before I made my final decision. On each occasion, when she appeared at my hotel room door, she acted as if we had never before met, lest an eavesdropper deduce that such rendezvous were common.

"So nice to meet you," she always said. "My company adheres to the highest standards and offers only trained and certified masseuses." Then, as she expertly rid my body of its many tensions, she again related her life story, each time adding two or three intriguing new details but never once suggesting that we had previously spoken.

Her unerring discretion convinced me at last that she was the perfect fulcrum about which my plan would turn.

★   ★   ★

9 September 1995—actually written one week hence.

A quiet Saturday morning in Great Falls. My unwitting Laotian infiltrator—whose working name was Janni—pranced up to the safehouse's tall wrought-iron gate and rang the bell. She was wearing a perfectly fitted pair of jeans, a clingy wool sweater, and construction-style designer boots. Her silky hair was pulled back in a simple ponytail, and her only makeup was a swath of subdued lipstick and a few strokes of mascara. From my vantage point, pressed as I was against the stone perimeter wall about one hundred feet away, Janni looked adorable, with an innocence and understated sensuality that reminded me of a fresh and perky college co-ed.

"May I help you?" crackled a disembodied voice from the intercom box. It was a native English speaker.

I was placing odds that this man was the lone obstacle between me and the murderer's throat. I'd debriefed enough defectors to know that the CIA usually assigned a single watcher to a safehouse, maintaining security with secrecy, stealth, anonymity, and mundanity, not with the brute strength of a large guard detail, which would certainly attract the neighbors' attention.

"This is Janni from Pink Orchid," she said. Her subtle accent was a mellifluous tribute to her mother tongue. "I have a delivery for"—she flipped through blank pages on a clipboard—"for a Mr. Park. Four adult videotapes. The order was placed by a Miss Betty Alvarez." Janni glanced up at the closed circuit camera and flashed a sigh-inducing smile.

I had told Janni that "Mr. Park" was a famous South Korean movie director and that Betty was his American publicist. Mr. Park, I had explained, greatly admired Southeast Asian beauty and would enjoy nothing more than a morning of watching Thai pornography while receiving an erotic massage. To maintain the famous director's reputation, I had continued, I would pay Janni five hundred dollars up front and another five hundred on completion of the session. Janni had readily agreed, which had come as no surprise, considering that her standard fee was either one or two hundred, depending on the services rendered.

The Security Officer's hesitant reply came after almost half a minute of quiet deliberation. "From Miss Alvarez? Uh, well, I guess.... Okay, sure, I suppose it would.... I'll buzz you in."

The latch emitted a faint click. Janni swung open the heavy gate and slipped into the compound.

I skulked over to the opening and crouched under the view of the camera. Then I reached out and caught the spring-loaded gate before it locked back into its jamb.

From my jacket pocket, I extracted my spyglass, which I'd used to case the UNJ terrorists' hideout in Egypt. The front of Pak's safehouse was nearby, but I wanted a magnified view to capture the nuances of Janni's interaction with the Security Officer.

The front door opened before Janni had a chance to knock. A muscular man about six feet tall stepped onto the porch and said, "Good morning. May I please see the tapes?" I knew that the Security Officer would have to inspect thoroughly any items before admitting them into the safehouse.

I twisted the lens of my spyglass and brought into sharp focus petite Janni, standing demurely with her feet together and her head tilted, gazing at the Security Officer as he rummaged through the cardboard box. He pulled out a brown-tinted glass bottle and said, "What's this?"

Janni peered down at her feet and said, "Body oil. I'm a trained and certified masseuse. Miss Alvarez also ordered my services for Mr. Park."

The Security Officer gazed at Janni for a moment, his eyes blinking slowly, and then he grinned. Through my telescope, I watched him look Janni over from head to toe. His expression hinted of animal hunger. He dropped the bottle into the box, which he handed back to Janni. "He's on the second floor," he told her, "first bedroom on the right."

As Janni brushed by him, the Security Officer reached out and grabbed her upper arm, stopping her on the safehouse's threshold. He said, "You've got forty-five minutes with him. When you and Romeo are finished, come back down and give me a sample of your *services*."

Janni nodded, pulled free, and scurried into the house.

I waited ten minutes before I put on a dark brown wig and donned the tinted spectacles that I'd last worn for the Kobayashi hit. I was also wearing the oversized suit from that same sojourn in Japan. The outfit made me look fifteen pounds lighter and ungainly, less of a threat.

I stood, threw open the gate, and charged toward the safehouse. The Security Officer must have seen me coming on one of the closed circuit cameras, for he swung open the front door and strode out to meet me, his right hand hidden behind him. I guessed that he was holding a pistol, probably the Agency standard issue, a Browning Hi-Power, the same model I'd used to perforate Sparrow leader Fenil Manag in the streets of Manila.

"You're trespassing, sir," the man said. "Please leave the property immediately."

"I followed my wife here," I said in a bad Spanish accent as I slowed to a walk. "What she's doing is forbidden by God, no matter how badly we need the money."

"Stop right there, please."

I complied and began wringing my hands. I furrowed my brow and gazed at the Security Officer with pleading eyes.

"Your wife's not here, amigo. Just me and my roommate."

I lowered my eyes. "Kind sir, I understand your embarrassment, but I followed her to your door. Her name is Janni, and she works for Pink Orchid. She promised me that her job involved only making deliveries, but now I know that she continues to...to touch other men." I jammed my hands into the suit's baggy pockets, sniffled, and shifted my weight from foot to foot, playing a man in emotional agony.

The Security Officer clenched his teeth, shook his head, and then cursed under his breath. "Wait right here," he said. He executed a smart about-face and took a step toward the door. The Security Officer should have known better than to turn his back on an intruder, no matter how harmless he—meaning I—seemed. I made him pay dearly for his sophomoric mistake.

From my right pants pocket I pulled a blackjack—a leather pouch filled with lead shot—and sprang at the man's back. He heard me coming and started to turn, but I slapped the blackjack against his head, behind his left ear. He crumpled silently to the porch. I noticed a pistol in a leather holster tucked into his waistband just behind his right hip.

I crouched over the man and felt for his neck pulse. Weak but steady. I ripped off my glasses and wig, then stood and dashed through the door. I located the stairs and quietly ascended to the second floor.

I pressed my ear to the first door and heard the unmistakable clamor of mating. I continued to listen and eventually discerned two discrete male voices, one recorded and the other live. Though this was far from Janni's first trick, I was still sickened by the thought of her quenching Pak's sordid thirsts.

I tested the handle; the door was unlocked. I pocketed the blackjack and in its place drew out a brand-new garrote. Then I burst into the bedroom.

Janni was pinned under Pak on the bed and seemed to be struggling against his advances. Her face brightened when she saw me. I was relieved that she was still wearing her undergarments—a brassiere and panties, bleached lace set in seductive contrast to her tawny skin.

"Hank!" she cried in a grateful tone. Perhaps she thought that at last a man was riding in on a white horse to liberate her from this vulgar servitude.

Pak leaped from the bed. He was stark naked and obviously aroused. His sinewy back bore a single smear of glistening oil. I surmised that he'd opted to skip the rest of the massage and get right down to the happy ending.

Pak began retreating toward the window, but I doubted he would leap from the second story. I stretched out my wire and, with great caution, advanced on my quarry. Still backing away, Pak bumped into the edge of the television, which was playing a noisy scene of Siamese ecstasy, and he glanced down to identify the obstacle. I took advantage of the momentary distraction and lunged forward.

With unexpected speed and agility, Pak squared off into what I recognized was a martial arts stance. As I was processing this information in mid-stride, Pak wound himself up and launched a spinning back-kick. The last thing I remember before hitting the floor was thinking that Pak had looked like a blurry little tornado.

A few seconds later I found myself face-down with the right side of my face already swelling and a taste of blood in my mouth. Pak was behind me, pummeling my kidneys. I had no idea where my garrote was and couldn't reach the blackjack in my pocket. Pak shifted forward and scooped an arm under my neck, putting me in a chokehold. Though I was gasping for precious air, I realized that my assailant had made a serious tactical mistake: Grappling was the domain of jujitsu, not tae kwon do.

I grabbed the back of Pak's hand, the one engaged in strangling me, and turned his wrist counterclockwise, pulling his thumb away from his body. Then I twisted his hand to the side, forcing his thumb down toward his arm's radius bone. He yelped and loosened his hold.

I rotated Pak's wrist a fraction more until it locked out, and then I unwrapped his arm from my neck and rolled onto my back. Maintaining my hold, I straightened Pak's arm with a violent yank and then thrust up into his elbow with my opposite palm, hyperextending the joint. With his entire arm now immobilized, I snapped Pak's wrist clockwise, flipping him onto the floor not six inches from where I'd just been prostrate. Then I drew his arm along the floor to a point above his head—as if I was setting the hand of a clock.

I shifted my grip and began pushing his palm down on his inner forearm. But in my zeal I applied too much force and his wrist collapsed with a cacophony of crunching bones.

Pak let out with an earsplitting shriek. But however painful and debilitating his injury, Pak's unhinged wrist meant that I no longer had him in a lock. He immediately began squirming around on the floor, denying me a better grip. As I fumbled with his injured arm, Pak corkscrewed under me and lashed out with his right elbow, striking me solidly in the sternum, knocking me onto my backside.

I looked up in time to see Pak draw back his right leg and fire a front snap kick into my solar plexus, deflating my lungs. My head bounced off the wall behind me, and I saw those familiar little stars, bright and shiny as ever.

Before I could clear my head, a battering ram was thrown against the left side of my head, and I felt as if my ear had been ripped off. As I watched the Milky Way swirl around in my mind's eye, I deduced that the talented Mr. Pak had just kicked me square in the head.

As on the streets of Rome, vomit came to my rescue. My stomach made a snap decision and emptied itself onto my lap. My vision cleared slightly, and then I retched again, this time projecting a yard-long aerosol stream onto Pak's bare feet, coating them with bile.

Pak stared at me and then at his feet, his face contorted by competing reactions—shock, outrage, horror, disgust. I noticed that his right arm was dangling by his side, the victim of my overly enthusiastic jujitsu attack.

Pak cocked his hips, preparing to fling another back kick, one that would've certainly ended the fight, but instead he slipped in a puddle of my stomach slime. My vomit was not a mere distraction; it was also an effective defense. Pak's legs whipped out from under him, and he went down hard on the flat of his back, his breath escaping the confines of his chest in a single massive cough.

I made several attempts to scramble to my feet, but I couldn't get my arms and legs to cooperate, each time bouncing back down on my rump. Meanwhile, Pak curled into a sitting position and hugged his knees. His respiration was still ragged but improving, and I knew that I had precious little time to prepare for our next skirmish.

I felt something small and flat under my right hand and turned to focus on it. A digital videodisk, a DVD, probably knocked out of the television cabinet during the scuffle. It was pornographic, of course, with lewd images stenciled on the exposed side. Grasping its edge, I snapped the disk in half against the floor.

I glanced over at my adversary. Using his good arm, he levered himself to his knees and glared back at me. I acted as if I were still dazed—eyelids aflutter, mouth agape. Pak grinned and snorted, obviously convinced that he could now make short work of me.

The North Korean rose to his feet and stared down at me. With uncertain and sluggish movements, I balled up my hands and covered my face, a feeble attempt, ostensibly, to protect myself from the looming onslaught. Pak chuckled, took two cautious steps forward, and leaned down, bringing his lips near my battered ear.

"Was your daddy or big brother on that airliner, little boy?" he whispered. "The plane I blew out of the sunny Bangkok sky?"

Still cowering, I peeked up at Pak through my fists. My arms were shaking—but not from fear.

"I'm honored," he said, "for the chance to kill another member of your family. I thought my retirement would deny me such pleasures."

As Pak spoke, I lowered my right hand two or three inches from my face, not enough for him to notice, but enough to end his life. I adjusted my weapon, extending it just beyond my thumb, and then drove my fist into Pak's larynx.

He jerked away from me, wrapping his hands around the wound. This time he did not scream; he could not scream. Blood oozed through Pak's fingers and soon formed a long red beard down his chest and abdomen. We locked gazes, and I smiled, holding up the bloody jagged half of the DVD that I'd just plunged into his throat.

Still staring at me, panic in his eyes, Pak sank to his knees and made clucking noises as his throat muscles tried in vain to force air down into his severed and seeping windpipe. His eyes crossed and rolled back into his head, and his hands went slack and released his neck. Then he toppled backward, pinning his feet under his buttocks.

Braced by a surge of adrenaline from my victory, I struggled to my feet and glanced around the ransacked room. Janni was sitting upright on the bed. Her face was pale, and her eyes were as big as saucers. She was traumatized, no doubt, from having just witnessed a very untidy duel to the death.

I limped over to Janni and stroked her smooth cheek with the back of my hand. She peered up at me and began to sob.

I pitied the girl, but I knew that the CIA Security Officer wouldn't stay unconscious forever. In the gentlest tone I could muster, I said, "Janni, please get dressed. We must get out of here before the police come."

My mention of "police" seemed to snap her back to her senses, for she climbed off the bed, retrieved her clothes from the top of a bureau, and slipped into them. I limped around the room until I'd found my garrote and blackjack—which had apparently been jettisoned during the brawl—and returned them to my pocket.

We exited together and alighted to the ground floor. At the landing, a shot rang out, and my right eye felt as if it had been stabbed with a red-hot poker. The blow threw me from my feet, and I landed on my back, with my poor bruised cranium bouncing off the bottom step. But this time, strangely, I saw no stars.

Whether time moved quickly or slowly I do not know. I only recall that I was staring up at the ceiling of the safehouse with my one good eye when Janni's concerned face appeared before me. She knelt down and started to weep, and I concluded that I must be in awfully bad condition. From behind Janni emerged the Security Officer, and he was holding a gorgeous Agency-issue Hi-Power.

My view of the world began to darken and contract. I felt Janni, who was still bawling, digging around in my pants pocket, and I wondered if she was looking for her second installment of five hundred dollars. But then she pulled out my blackjack and slipped her hand through its leather strap. If my mouth had worked, I would've cheered.

She stood, spun around, and hammered the weapon into the Security Officer's forehead. He disappeared instantly from my ever-shrinking viewfinder.

Janni knelt back down and said, "I'll run up the road and get your car. Don't try to move. I promise I'll be back."

A few seconds later, I left God's flawed but still majestic world with a childhood prayer echoing in my broken head. These simple words I had whispered every night while my dear mother watched over me:

*Now I lay me down to sleep,*
*I pray the Lord my soul to keep.*
*And if I die before I wake,*
*I pray the Lord my soul to take....*

# 21

# BUCCANEER

Lucky seven divides three times into twenty-one, and twenty-one wins at blackjack, a card game that shares its name with the weapon that saved my life. Sentimentality compelled me to keep the garrote at the top of my list, but the blackjack has now moved into a close and most honorable second place.

★ ★ ★

With my spy career in ruins, I decided to try my hand at piracy, but with a twist: I would prey only on the sea's most ruthless freebooters, performing virtuous services as a privateer-hunter, a marauder of marauders. After years of pursuing equity while in the employ of the wayward CIA, I felt well qualified to assume a seemingly sullied title for the purpose of achieving a noble goal.

Besides, buccaneering was one of the few professions in which an eye patch was an acceptable fashion accessory.

From my hammock in the tree line, I could see Irene ambling toward me along the beach, cradling Henry with one arm. She was wearing a marvelous neon-green string bikini. Hardly a day passed—especially when she was so attired—that I failed to recall my sublime evenings with her on Mount Athena.

When Irene came within earshot, I called out in my familiar way: "I see England, I see France, I see Irene's underpants!"

"With only one eye," she answered, "you're fortunate you can see anything at all."

As I ogled Irene's sumptuous passing, I was visited by another memory, this one not so pleasant as my reverie about trysts on Mount Athena.

After I was shot in the head, Janni had returned and somehow loaded me into—and later out of—my car. Perhaps I'd been momentarily ambulatory and able to provide some degree of helpful locomotion. Either that or Janni had found reserves of strength and ingenuity beyond my capacity for conjecture.

I eventually awakened with a jolt, bathed in an ice-cold sweat, wondering where the hell I was and how long I'd been there. (Janni was to tell me later that I'd been comatose for six and a half days.)

I found myself in an expansive bed in a nicely appointed room. I tilted my waterlogged head to the right and slowly brought Janni into focus. She was curled up next to me, smiling.

I finally realized that I was seeing with only my left eye, so I used my fingers to explore the damage. Almost my entire head—except for the left side of my face and my mouth—was swathed in bandages, which made my braincase roughly the size and shape of a prize pumpkin at the county fair.

I looked again at beaming Janni and then over at the bedside table, which was littered with small medicine bottles and disposable syringes. A clear plastic bag hung on the bedpost over my head.

"Painkillers and antibiotics," Janni said. "The bag is for saline and sometimes glucose."

Still feeling my way through a post-cataleptic fog, I was startled, and perhaps a little unsettled, by Janni's resourcefulness and familiarity with the practice of medicine. I was beginning to realize that it was no fluke she'd survived the long and arduous journey from a Laotian village to a Thai brothel to the Maryland suburbs.

"Thanks," I said, my voice cracking.

Janni produced a glass of water and tipped it toward my lips. My first swallows were painful, but once a trail was blazed down my arid throat, I drank in large gulps until the glass was empty.

Thus fortified, I finally noticed that Janni was wearing a translucent pink teddy. Even in my weakened state, I found her apparel most captivating.

★　　★　　★

22 September 1995.

After another week of steady improvement, I signed over my car's title to Janni and said, "Get what you can for it, then buy a roundtrip ticket for me to Manila, with a departure in three or four weeks." I handed her a scrap of paper. "Use this name."

She read the note and pursed her lips. "Who's Ahmed Elliot El-Gamal?"

"I need my jacket," I said, pointing toward the closet where my clothes hung.

Janni, dressed in another skimpy negligee, retrieved my rumpled suit, and I ripped out a section of the coat's lining. I extracted a British passport and a silver credit card, and held the items out to Janni. She took them, flipped open the passport, and gasped.

"It's you," she said, "with dark hair and eyes."

"Mr. El-Gamal is the key to my escape."

Janni took this odd revelation without batting an eye. "I'll use the credit card to guarantee your reservations," she said, "and you can pay in cash at the counter when the ticket is issued."

* * *

Janni never asked why I had a foreign passport in an assumed name. So I never needed to explain to her how, after being recalled from Rome, I'd turned in only part of my alias-document packages to a gawky clerk in the CIA's Europe Division, more commonly known as E-U-R.

As I relinquished each bundle of papers and pocket litter, the receiving officer, at most twenty years old and with an Adam's apple the size of a billiard ball, paused just long enough to scratch a checkmark on a mustard-stained computer printout. For the El-Gamal persona, I submitted my Cypriot documents but kept the British set secreted in my jacket, where it would stay unless the clerk asked directly for it.

The Agency, I well knew, rarely issued two passports for one alias. I put down a bet that this baby-faced bookkeeper, so obviously splashed with the colognes of inexperience and indifference, would process me without taking the time to do his research.

And in that spin of the big wheel, I came out the winner.

★   ★   ★

21 October 1995.

Six weeks after the shooting, I lathered my skin with tanning cream, dyed my hair and eyebrows, and inserted one brown contact lens. I pecked Janni on the cheek and, despite her protests, pushed into her hands an envelope filled with cash—what was left of the ten thousand dollars she'd gotten for my car. Then I told her to forget that she ever knew me, watched a single tear slide down her smooth face, and shuffled out of her apartment to the waiting taxi out front.

I consumed eight codeine tablets on the long flight to Manila. My head throbbed with pain the entire trip. I often considered the possibility that I might be forever plagued with such bouts of agony, thanks to the lead slug that was lodged behind what had once been my right eye.

After I disembarked into Ninoy Aquino International Airport, I immediately found a pay phone and rang up PNP Lieutenant Manny Rodriguez, my former agent Destrier.

"Manny, it's Hank. Just arrived. Need you to pull me out of line into secondary for a 'random' docs check." I plucked out and threw aside the contact lens. "My hair's dark brown, I'm sporting one hell of a tan, and I'm wearing a baggy tweed suit. Oh yeah—and an eye patch."

This was how Hank Anlaf arrived in the Philippines four days before the raid on Pak Sang-Il's safehouse in Great Falls. The immigration stamp in my true name passport—which Janni had sewn into my jacket lining for my departure from Washington-Dulles airport—and back-dated entries in the NAIA and airline-reservation databases proved that I'd been swinging in my hammock on Sparta when turncoat Pak met his demise.

My watertight alibi cost me the customary bottle of single-malt and five bills. And as a bonus, Manny fed my El-Gamal documents into the growling shredder in his office.

★　★　★

25 October 1995.

I rode a ferryboat from Manila to Agutaya, the capital of the Cuyo Islands, and then hired a native outrigger to take me to Pawikan/Sparta. I'd chosen these modes of transport because sea vessels in the Philippines kept no passenger manifests.

I found the island severely depopulated; only three ladies and baby Henry had remained behind. Irene, concerned by my ugly wound and emaciated body, immediately took up the role as my personal nurse. Vivacious Imelda, my life's new love, and scrawny but cheerful Giuliana signed on as Irene's eager assistants. With the help of these wonderful women, I recovered fully in two months, with my migraines decreasing in frequency to about five controllable episodes a quarter.

Little Henry was now the island's titular boy-king, the acknowledged heir to the throne of Sparta. I occupied a position as first among equals on the Council of Elders, together with Irene and Imelda. Giuliana, the last migrant to reach Sparta's shores, was promoted to the One and Only Overseer.

We all knew that Henry would grow to see the end of Sparta's lease and would be responsible for the island's return to the Cuyo Islands Fishermen's Federation. But, as Irene informed me, the locals considered Henry a native and had invited him to remain on Sparta for as long as he so desired.

As for me, I was determined to live out my days in our tiny empire, in the company of good friends and my godson, and to pass the time mounting offensives against the filthy picaroons of the Sulu Sea. Here I would commission the building of another scaled-down Viking longboat, this one polished and seaworthy and equipped with a powerful inboard engine and automatic weapons.

And when the final curtain is dropped on my audacious life, I shall be buried in my dragon boat on the summit of Mount Athena, next to my dear friend Stan. On that welcome day, we two unrepentant cads will march side by side through Valhalla, with my eye and Stan's legs restored, praising "no sword until tested, no maid until bedded, no ice until crossed, no ale until drunk."*

---

* A quote from the Ninth Century Viking poem *Havamal*.

CPSIA information can be obtained at www.ICGtesting.com
Printed in the USA
LVOW060103160812

294556LV00001B/180/A